A Latte to Die For

Book 3: Crystal Creek Mysteries

By M. Sue Alexander

M. Sue Alexander

This book is a work of fiction. Names and characters in the story are a product of the author's imagination. Any resemblance to actual persons, living or dead, events or locales, is coincidental. Should you purchase a copy of this book without a cover, be aware this book may be stolen property and neither the publisher nor the author has received payment for a "stripped book."

Book 3

FIRST EDITION 2022, USA
SUZANDER PUBLISHING

Copyright © 2022 by M. Sue Alexander

All rights reserved by author. No part of this book may be reproduced in any form, either by electronic or mechanical means, including information storage and retrieval systems, without obtaining written permission from the publisher, except by a reviewer who may quote brief passages in a review. Scripture quotations are from *The Living Bible*. Copyright © 1971, Tyndale House Publishers; Wheaton, Illinois 60187, and used by permission. All rights reserved.

Book Cover by Christine Roszak

**View M. Sue's Website and Facebook Page
www.msuealexanderbooks.com**

A Latte to Die For

Series Titles by Author

Resurrection Dawn 2014 Series

Book 1: Resurrection Dawn 2014 *Book 2:* The Christian Fugitive
Book 3: Rebels in Paradise   *Book 4:* Veil of Lies
Book 5: The Anointing   *Book 6:* Countdown to Justice
Book 7: All Rise   *Book 8:* Unlikely Suspect
Book 9: Lethal Snapshot   *Book 10:* Purgatory
Book 11: April Fool's Day   *Book 12:* Reign of Errors

Time of Jacob's Trouble

Book 1: The Four Horsemen   *Book 2:* Beast
Book 3: Witness   *Book 4:* The Word
Book 5: Judgment   *Book 6:* Deceiver
Book 7: False Prophet   *Book 8:* Satan
Book 9: The Image
Book 10: Jesus the Appearance

Crystal Creek Mysteries

Book 1: Two Dead on Crystal Creek
Book 2: Poison Tea

Independent Titles

Adam's Bones
Encounters of the God-Kind
Grandma's Coming (children's book)
Out of Time: The Vanderbilt Incident
The Forum
The Minister's Haunting
Tomorrow's Promise

M. Sue Alexander

1

Monday, May 8

"GG, WHY DOES MAMA say you're always getting into trouble?"

Mama is my granddaughter, Helen, June's mother. Helen is married to Patrick Lancaster, a CPA by profession. June's younger brother is William but we call him Billy. I can barely keep up with everybody's birthday with gifts and cards. Such is old age.

This day has just begun as I look at my five-year-old great-granddaughter and sweetly smile. "What do you mean by that, June?"

I think I already know, but I want to hear her answer.

"Well, MM says you like trouble."

These kids, they have capital letters for everything they talk about. I blame it on the internet, the text formats that lure children into the social world so they can find out everything they shouldn't know.

"I presume MM stands for *My Mother*?"

June nods. "MD says it sometimes, too."

My Daddy. "Look, June. Your Great Grandmother has no time for such nonsense. Shouldn't you be getting dressed for school?"

I need to stop this foolish line of thinking. As long as I keep my mouth shut, I'm not in trouble. I'm wonderful. I've sold my farm with my lovely remodeled house in late February to Ellie Simpson and her devoted parents and they are divinely happy. They moved into the house in early March and I became Lorene Perkin's guest, planning only to stay a week. Except a week had not panned out. What happened two months ago on Thursday, March 9, changed everything.

≈

A bright spring morning had dawned on March 13. I was seated in Lorene's kitchen at the bar with a mug of coffee in one hand and the morning newspaper in the other when mayhem struck.

Lorene's cell phone rings and she answers it.

At first, she listens with a smile. Then her expression turns dark as she frowns. That caused a moment of concern. I point my finger at her phone, then my right ear, signaling for her to turn on the speaker so I can hear what is being said. But she does not and waves me off.

Somehow, I sense nothing good would come from this call. So, I wait impatiently for a bad report. Lorene ends the call and lays the phone on the counter, sighing. She looks at me like I have the answers.

"Who died?" I immediately ask.

"Gloria Ann Bolton. Stroke."

"What?" We'd just had coffee with her last week. Thursday, I believe. Today is Monday, five days ago. Who was on the phone?"

"Gerry, he wants to see us."

"Now, why? We didn't cause her stoke."

"Are you sure?" Lorene says with a tremble in her voice.

Suddenly, I feel troubled and cornered. I try to remember what I'd said to my former high school classmate. A woman I instinctively disliked. She'd dated my Arthur before I did and was my rival in high school. Lorene's comment has shaken me to the core.

"Surely, Gerry jests," I tell Lorene.

"I don't think so, Dorothy."

Now I'm frowning, and now I'm worried.

"Did he say what I might have said to upset Gloria?"

This feels like a he-said-she-said conversation that will get us nowhere. I sigh, more poignantly than Lorene did when she'd heard the bleak news. "We should go and talk to Gerry."

"I have to shower and dress first," Lorene says.

"Me, too. Call Gerry back and tell him we'll meet him at the Senior Citizen Center in one hour." I go upstairs to get ready.

We ride into town in Lorene's pea-green Tesla. The price of gas at the pump makes me wish I'd purchased a Hybrid vehicle instead of my gas-guzzling red BMW, now only two years old.

It's still early for most elderly citizens of Columbia to be arriving for the discounted senior lunch, thanks to Big Brother who wants to influence our votes when it comes to public elections. Whether Democrats or Republicans, they all have bucks in the basket.

Lorene drives so slowly it makes me crazy. I think of Claire who drives too fast, and how upset she'll be when I tell her I can't move to Nashville yet. She wants me to buy a condo close to her house.

Theodore, Ted to those in our family, is still involved with the music business, managing the investments of popular country- western music stars. He used to represent only males, not anymore.

I suspect Claire is jealous when he takes a good-looking younger artist out for drinks to discuss business investments. Sometimes he comes home with perfume on his shirt collar. Suspicious, if you ask me. But my daughter loves and trust him. Her failure, I fear.

I try to focus on the moment.

"You're mighty quiet, my friend," Lorene tells me.

"Just meandering thoughts, not worth mentioning." I think of Thomas Kessler and miss him terribly. The Christmas card he sent me postmarked from Moscow, Russia, haunts me since I have no confirmation he lives. So, the ghost of what was stirs my memories.

Then I think he might show up any day. He always was a mystery. CIA through and through. What would I do? Run away with him?

Why not? We have a history. I resemble his murdered wife Angela, though she's a good fifteen years younger than me. Tom took a bullet for me. Who does that unless they care for someone deeply?

Lorene pulls her pea-green Tesla into a parking space on court square and we get out. It's chilly outdoors, windy like March always is, but the sun shines and its warmth soaks through my sweater.

Lorene has her hand on the door knob before I stop her.

"Wait! Do you recall anything we said to Gloria that may have upset her?" I truly could not remember one missaid word.

"Other than *you* told her she needed a facelift."

"Oh, that!" I threw my hand. "I was only teasing."

"She didn't think you were." Lorene's hand is still on the knob.

"Please don't tell Gerry I said that."

"Maybe he already knows. Do you want me to lie?"

I suddenly feel alone in the universe. My best friend seems to want to distance herself from me—like I somehow killed Gloria with my suggestion that she should get a facelift. I try to recall what she'd said to me that prompted my ugly response. Oh, it was, "You should try my new Botox formula to get rid of some of your wrinkles."

"No, I don't want you to lie, Lorene. Just don't bring it up unless Gerry does. Okay? I don't want to upset him even more. He just lost the love of his life, if you really believe that is possible."

Lorene drops her hand from the doorknob.

"What?" I feel a chill from the brisk wind.

"Wasn't Arthur the love of your life? You were married to him for fifty years. Or is Tom the love of your life?"

I frown. "That was mean, Lorene. Tom is gone and I'll never see him again. Yes, I care deeply for him, but he was too young for me." I glare at her, daring her to dig deeper into my feelings.

"So true, now that we're being honest."

Does Lorene think I am lying?

"Look, are we enemies now?" I ask.

"I'm on truth's side," Lorene declares, like she owns justice.

The door opens and we see a bleary-eyed Gerry Bolton. "Come in ladies, you'll catch a death in this chilly wind."

"If one thing doesn't get us another will," I mutter under my breath, angry with Lorene and feeling our friendship falling apart.

Why does everything keep changing? I'll be eighty-three in June. I want to live a quiet, uneventful life, for the rest of my days. I want Arthur to greet me on St. Peter's front porch and walk through the door with me. I want to see Tom one more time on this side of Heaven. But life is not always a bowl of cherries, I realize.

We enter the large hall and sit down at a rectangular table, Gerry on one side, Lorene and I across from him. I won't start the conversation. But he does. And I hope I can survive today.

"Gloria came home out of sorts after she met you for coffee." He glares at me. I want to say Lorene was there, too. The silence is loud.

I touch Lorene's hand under the table. *Your turn.*

"Oh. When did she pass?" Lorene softly inquires.

"Not until late Sunday," Gerry replies, sniffling. "I could tell she was feeling awful, but she wouldn't let me call the doctor."

"You should have anyway, Gerry," I barge in.

"In hindsight, I should have. But Gloria doesn't even take high-blood pressure medicine. I thought she'd picked up a bug."

"Maybe she did," I speculate. "She ordered a jellied croissant."

"Gloria doesn't eat fattening food; she watches her figure."

I bet you do, too, I thought, but didn't speak it out.

Lorene is quiet as a church mouse like she's in the middle of a fiery sermon. I want to scream at her: HELP ME OUT, FRIEND!

Gerry continues, "She passed out around 8:30 last night and I called an ambulance to take her to the hospital. She died on the way."

"We're so sorry." I include Lorene in my remark of empathy.

"Why do you want to talk to us, Gerry?" Lorene asks.

"After Gloria met you at Coffee Call on Thursday, she came home feeling a bit nauseous and out of sorts." He glares at me again. "Did either of you say something to upset my wife?"

I feel the tyranny of his remark and will defend myself.

"Maybe it wasn't *us* that upset Gloria," I retort. "Maybe something happened on her way home that made her feel out of sorts. Maybe she stopped at a fast-food restaurant and bought a tainted burger."

He frowns. "Like I said, Gloria doesn't eat fattening foods."

"Maybe she was poisoned," I blurt out. "Did you do it, Gerry?"

"Dorothy!" Lorene exclaims in horror, half standing and swinging a hand that knocks over Gerry's big ceramic mug of coffee. It splatters in his lap, all over his white shirt, and drips off the table on the floor like an exploding grenade. I wonder how this day can get any worse.

"Sorry," Lorene apologizes, leaning across the table to smear the coffee stain even further over his expensive shirt with a Kleenex.

"It's okay, Lorene, my shirt will wash." He glares at me.

I feel the need to defend myself further.

"Did you take out a large insurance policy on Gloria that pays at the time of her death?" I query. "My Arthur took one out on himself and named me as his beneficiary. I was accused of murdering him."

Lorene says, "That is totally uncalled for, Dorothy."

I don't care, I am mad. I'm not everyone's enemy.

Gerry is flabbergasted, doesn't know what to say. If he expects me to apologize for upsetting his wife when she started it on Thursday, he will wait until Hell freezes over. I am not responsible for Gloria's death and he won't lay that burden on me. He will not point a finger at me.

No way, Hosea! I glare back at him, my stance firm.

"It's not the same thing, Dorothy," Gerry says in a calmer voice. "I'm not accusing either of you of doing anything that caused Gloria's death. But I'd like to know everything that was said over coffee."

I look at Lorene. "I don't remember everything said."

Lorene's lips are clamped. She's shaking her head.

"What do you recall, Lorene?" Gerry asks, like I would lie.

"We talked about the Spring Ball you have planned for our senior citizens," she begins. "Dorothy told her about selling her house to Ellie Simpson in February and, you know, just women's stuff."

I'm glad Lorene put it that way. *Women's stuff* includes Gloria's suggestion I take Botox treatments and my response that she should consider getting a facelift. But none of that is a crime.

Trust me, I know criminal activity. . .

I realize June is speaking to me.

"What, dear?" I snap out of my reverie.

"Are you having a senior moment, GG?"

"Where did you hear that?" I inquire.

"On TV. You can take Viagra for that."

I chuckle. "No, June, that's for another thing."

"What thing?"

"Ask MM, she'll explain."

"Is a senior moment like pulling a memory stick out of a computer?" June is bent on an educational response.

"Yes, only the stick is in my brain powering up stuff that gets in the way by bringing up memories from the past," I explain.

"GG, that's too hard for me, I'm only in kindergarten."

"I know, June. I feel the same way."

Claire comes down the stairs to the den. "Your mother will be here in five minutes, June, and you're not even dressed."

"I've been busy, MMM. GG is teaching me about Viagra."

My Mother's Mother?

"Have a nice day at school, June," I tell her, put on my jacket, pick up my purse, and scoot on out of the house. I'd rather be driving around in my BMW than explaining my unorthodox conversation with my great granddaughter. Some things are best left unsaid.

Let June ask MM about my senior moment.

My daughter trails me to the front door.

"Mama? What was that all about?"

"Bye, Claire. I'll be spending the day with Lorene, and probably tonight. So don't plan on me for supper." I wave as leave the house.

2

I STOP FOR A DUNKIN Donuts' latte on my way to Columbia, so I do not arrive at Lorene's house until close to 8:30 a.m. She is standing on the front porch in anticipation of my arrival. I can always tell by her expression when she has something important on her mind.

"What is it now?" I ask as soon as we stand face to face.

"Detective Galena Chico is looking for you."

"I don't know any Chico, except the clothing company that sells fantastic creative jewelry." I brush past her with my overnight case.

"You can't ignore the truth any longer, Dorothy."

I turn around in the doorway and give her a discriminant look.

"Truth has many facets," I express my opinion.

"Better think twice about that!" Lorene calls out then trails me through the foyer and den and up the stairs where I deposit my overnight case in her guest bedroom. This place feels more like home than Claire's. "Avoidance can get you in big trouble."

"Why should it? Truth does not always need to be told."

"It does if a detective asks you."

Lorene leers at me from the doorway.

"Okay, you win." The breath sucks out of me like a deflating flat tire. "Did this Chico person leave a phone number?"

"Yes, it's the same office number that Butch had," Lorene states.

Butch is the nickname of Columbia's former lead detective. Lloyd Peters was murdered on Thanksgiving Day and his apartment burnt to a crisp. No forensic evidence was ever found that pointed a finger at the creep who shot him in the back and stole his life. Butch was engaged to Ellie Simpson. There was nothing I could do about all that.

"Did you get breakfast yet?" Lorene asks as we descend the stairs to her kitchen. I see a pan of cinnamon rolls sitting on the counter.

"Not enough that I won't try one of those delicious pastries."

"Help yourself, Dorothy."

I've lost another fifteen pounds since Christmas, mostly due to mooning over Thomas Kessler. He could at least phone me.

I gather a couple of rolls and place them on a paper plate then nuke them for twenty seconds. The hint of cinnamon spice suffuses the kitchen, accommodating the dripping coffee odor in its maker.

She watches me while I complete my task.

"Are you spending the night with me?" Lorene leans over the kitchen bar, close enough for me to smell her bacon breath.

"Where else would I stay?" I munch on a roll and my stomach growls with delight. Lorene is an excellent cook. I rarely bake anymore since I am homeless. "Have you talked to Alicia recently?"

The elderly Alicia Colby from England previously lived in Clyde Willems' old cabin three miles behind the house I used to own.

"Yesterday." Lorene fills two green mugs with coffee then adds sugar and cream to both. She knows how I like mine. Like Tom did.

"How is she adjusting to her living quarters?" Steam rises from my mug so I wait a bit for it to cool while I finish off a roll.

"She likes her independent living unit. And her association with other seniors and social activities provide plenty of entertainment."

Lorene usually picks Alicia up on Fridays and takes her to the Senior Citizen Center for lunch. Someone else takes her home before our card game commences at two. I play as often as I can.

"Are you playing cards with us this week?" Lorene asks.

"Of course, I'm here. Why do you ask?" I stare at Lorene.

"Jane wants to know for sure."

Jane Murphy and Elizabeth Hinson are our canasta partners.

"Why? Is she anxious to replace me?" I take exception.

"Who knows? Jane is really weird sometimes."

Lorene chuckles as if the idea is funny. It's not to me.

"Well, as long as I'm a citizen of Tennessee, you can tell Jane I am playing Canasta with my friends every Friday afternoon in Columbia."

I will not be excluded or dismissed so easily.

"Let's take our coffees in the den," Lorene suggests.

I abandon my second cinnamon roll and trail Lorene. She plops down in Crawford's old recliner while I sink my skinny butt into the sofa. "So, what did Detective Chico say exactly when she called you?"

"You should talk to her," Lorene says.

"I'm talking to you."

"I don't want to misquote her."

"That bad, huh?"

Lorene's mouth is clamped tighter than a clam's shell.

"Okay." I remove my cell phone from my pocket and dial the same number I've called dozens of times before the new year came.

Lorene glares at me as the airways pick up my call and transfer it to a cell tower, then onto the exact number of the recipient. I wait, feeling under the eye of a microscope. I know what I did and it could look pretty bad for me if something lethal was in that cup of coffee.

"She's not answering." I end the call.

"Why didn't you leave a message, Dorothy?"

"I didn't want to." I trot into the kitchen for my second cinnamon roll. I am going to need all the comfort of calories I can get today.

We spend most of the morning planting flower bulbs in the garden spot next to Lorene's back patio. I am knee deep in dirt so I take a shower and get dressed. We're eating lunch out.

Around eleven thirty, I pull into the parking lot of a brand-new senior-living complex that features independent, assisted, and nursing home choices of residences. Miss Alisha Colby is ninety-two, but can still walk and think. She enjoys having meals at the community dining room and having a maid clean her one-bedroom unit twice a week.

That could be an option for me, but I'm not ready yet.

Lorita Willems, Clyde Willems' half-sister, gifted Alicia his old cabin behind my house soon after he was murdered by the same man that killed my Arthur. Alicia remodeled the cabin, gave it a facelift, and turned it into a work of art. I am reminded that I have an appointment with Dr. Sharra tomorrow. I want to look younger if I see Tom again.

The touch of a button kills the BMW motor and I glare at Lorene.

She sits quietly in the passenger seat, not making eye contact, and not having said two words since I informed her that I intended to speak directly to the Medical Examiner. I cannot stand that my so-called best friend is uncomfortable discussing my dilemma.

"I swear, my friend, you'd think I'd committed the unpardonable sin." Still, no response, and that's worrisome. "Talk to me, Lorene."

"Well, Dorothy . . ." she turns half way in her seat, "maybe you should talk to Graham before you rush over to see Cynthia."

"Why?"

"He can clear the way for you."

Cynthia is Lorene's daughter-in-law, Graham's new wife. She's also the Medical Examiner for Maury County and autopsied Gloria Bolton's body. The results have not become public yet, but I want to know what caused Gloria's death before I talk to Detective Chico and explain what occurred the day Lorene and I had coffee with Gloria.

"Do you think I need clearing?" I ask.

"I'm worried that something bad was in her coffee."

"*My* coffee, you mean."

"Yes, your coffee—the cup you switched with Gloria."

"And if she got sick because of it, I'm too blame? What if I got sick?" I suddenly realize if a lethal substance caused Gloria's stroke, and I was served the coffee, then the dose of death was meant for me.

"Someone possibly tried to kill me, Lorene!"

"Don't assume that until we know for sure."

"Well, I'd say Gloria's death pretty much seals that coffin."

Lorene shakes her head. "That was pretty harsh, Dorothy."

"Okay, let's talk to Graham at Walgreen's right after we take Alicia to a nice lunch then deposit her safely back at the facility."

"It's a plan." Lorene opens the passenger door and gets out.

3

AS WE PASS THE FIRESTATION, Lorene spies her younger son Sam standing in the driveway. "Stop the car, Dorothy!"

"Why?" I wonder, since we are on our way to Walgreens to see Graham. Lorene leaps out of the car and rushes over to Sam.

The doors to the fire station yawn wide open and the fire engine is lit up like a singing Christmas tree. I watch amazed at how all the handsome young men in their tectonic fireproof garments carry body gear that weighs possibly more than I do. The crew is about to leave to fight a fire somewhere. Yet, Lorene doesn't seem to notice.

I park on the street and get out of the car.

"Excuse me, Sam." Lorene approaches and taps him on the shoulder. At first, he ignores her then swings around.

I observe a flicker of anger turn to concern.

"Mama, now is not the time."

"My question will only take a few seconds," she says.

"Time to go, Sam," one of his buddies calls out.

"Call me later!" He walks away.

"Wait!" Lorene stands there long enough for me to worry.

"Come on, Lorene," I call out, "he's busy."

She tramps over to me. "That was rude."

"It's his job, honey." I know her feelings are hurt.

The fire engine captain calls out to board, like any ship master ready to haul out on an adventure. As the brave men attach themselves to the side of the red engine, we step out of the way to avoid getting run over. And away they go, sirens screaming so loud I have to place my hands over my ears. Lorene watches in defeat.

"What was so urgent that you had to talk to him right then?"

"I wanted to tell him he left his jacket at my house," she replies.

"Lorene, that isn't urgent. You should call him."

"I know, but he was right there."

"Okay, friend," I give her a hug, "Let's go talk to Graham." I pray he won't brush her off like Sam just did. Mothers expect to be a priority—be damned the job! We walk back to my car and get in.

"Forget about Graham, Dorothy. Let's go see Cyn and tell her what you did. Maybe she'll share Gloria's autopsy report."

"Worth a try!" And off we go to challenge the wizard of forensic data trapped in dead bodies. I suspect it's a waste of time, but I'll do almost anything to avoid talking to Detective Galena Chico today.

The Medical Examiner's office is located ten blocks from the fire station in the basement of an antiquated private three-story hospital. Upper floors house elderly patients with advanced mental conditions.

"I sure hope they aren't saving a room for me up there," Lorene comments and I pull into a space marked GUEST. The elderly fear deterioration of their minds even more than their physical parts.

"If you had Alzheimer's, you would know it by now." I put the BMW in park and we get out. I lock my doors with my car fob.

We enter the front door of the building. I look up and notice a camera pointed our way and suspect we've just had our portraits taken.

"What if Cynthia is busy, too?" I punch the LL button for Lower Level next to the elevator doors. I'm not in the mood for what the morgue may offer a floor below us. But . . . it is what it is.

"Cyn is always here, it's her job—twenty-four-seven," Lorene says as we descend in the shaky old vault built seventy-five years ago. Its sides are ceramic blocks and the floors are so dirty I can't tell what we're stepping on. The elevator trembles in progress, not unlike my stomach. Lorene has her watchful eyes glued on me.

"What?" I react. "So, I'm a little nervous."

"My daughter-in-law is a professional, she'll level with us."

That's what I fear, although I won't voice it.

We exit the elevator and the odor of formaldehyde mingled with death greets us like the Grim Reaper on Halloween. I want to puke.

A guy is walking toward us. Skinny and tall, his complexion is a pasty white and dented on the sides of his tight mouth. He stops in front of us. Actually, he blocks our way. Who is he guarding?

"What can we do for you today, ladies?"

His voice is husky for a young fellow and he has a bad case of acne. His badge says GORDY. Obviously, a nickname for Gordon.

"I'm here to see my daughter-in-law," Lorene pipes, using her clout to get us a quick interview. "Is she here?"

Gordy's parched lips twist to the left. "Yeah, probably still in her office." He turns around and points down the long hallway.

"And if she isn't?" I pose.

"She'll be in the autopsy room. I don't recommend you go in there without wearing proper equipment. It's a Covid-death case."

I lock eyes with Lorene. "We won't!" It's a unanimous decision.

The hallway seems endless, and I think of Arthur's journey into the Light after he stared Death in the face. I cannot fathom what it will feel like to die, but chances are I won't have to wait too many years to find out. If only we could find a way to leave behind a note for those who are still breathing. I sigh. All of this is useless speculation.

"Oh!" Dr. Cynthia Perkins yelps as Lorene bumps into her as she comes out of her office. "Mama, what are you doing here?"

The question is for Lorene but Cyn is glaring at me.

"We have a question, it won't take long," Lorene explains.

Cyn nods. "Okay, three minutes. Come in, ladies."

We trail the M.E. into her compact office and spy dozens of manila folders on her desk, several of them open with its guts spilling out. Stories of the deaths of people I may know. We stand and wait.

"What is it, Mama?" Cyn seems impatient to get on with her work.

"Dorothy needs to know what killed Gloria Bolton."

The M.E.'s cinnamon eyes query me as a golden curl slips loose from her cap. "I'm not a liberty to publicly release that information."

"It's not public, Cyn, it's for me and Dorothy," Lorene argues.

The new bride has put on a little weight since marrying Graham last year. I wonder if she's pregnant. It's not my place to ask.

Cyn places her hands on Lorene's shoulder. "Mama, I'd tell you if I could. You know that. It's not my place to make that decision."

I know Cyn's right. Lorene has put her on the spot on my behalf. She loves me like a sister. If I could only be certain the coffee Gloria consumed did not contribute to her death, telling Detective Chico that I switched cups with her would not be necessary. I want to be sure.

"Mama, I just can't." Cyn looks directly at me. "Talk to Detective Chico. If she decides to divulge the autopsy report, I have no problem with that." Silence follows. "Meanwhile, I have work to do."

I nod. "Thank you, anyhow." *For nothing*, I think to myself.

Cyn activates her cell phone and makes a call. A few minutes later, the same guy we met in the hall appears. "This way out, ladies."

We're out on the street again.

"Well, that was useless," I declare.

"Now are you ready to go and see Detective Chico?"

"What choice do I have?"

We drive over to the same building that housed Detective Lloyd Peters' office, pass the same guy Jake at the desk, take the same elevator up to the second floor, and walk through the same office door.

Ellie Simpson is not sitting at her desk. A guy is. He looks like he just graduated from high school, but I feel sure he has a degree in secretarial skills. "Is Detective Chico busy?" Lorene approaches him.

I linger near the door, so I can run if I have to.

"Her door is shut," he mouths. "That means she's busy."

"We'll wait," I decide and plop my butt in a chair. I'm not leaving until I settle this matter. Did I actually murder Gloria Bolton?

4

WE HAD BEEN SITTING IN Detective Galena Chico's office for more than thirty minutes before she opens the door to her private domain. Her gaze swallows me. The newest detective in town is a beautiful creature. Her Latino genes have matured with her years on earth. Eyes huge and black as mysterious universes are orbs of starlight. Her lips are plump and pink, and I wonder how many good-looking men have kissed them. Am I jealous of youth and beauty? You bet.

But I once had my time, I remind myself.

"Can I help you, ladies?" she inquires.

"I am Dorothy Powell. You were looking for me."

I'm so proud of myself I'm actually smiling. I've bravely announced, "Here I am, what are you going to do with me?"

"You must be Lorene Perkins." Chico shakes her hand then turns to me. "Thank you for coming in, Mrs. Powell."

"We started to phone first, but decided it was better to talk in person." I wonder if this encounter is truly wise. Lying to a person's face is much harder than over the phone. But here I am, so be it.

"I just have a few questions to clear up," Chico says. "Let's talk in my office." She points at her secretary. "Blake, hold my calls."

"Yes, ma'am," he respectfully replies.

The door is closed to the office and I see no way of escape. Detective Chico's office has one window that looks down on the street. I recall sitting in this same chair in October more than two years ago, getting grilled by Detective "Butch" Peters. He actually accused me of murdering Arthur. But the truth eventually surfaced.

Chico takes a seat at her desk and leans back in the swiveling office chair, ergonomic I suspect. "Do either of you recognize the name Danny Mason?" She sits upright and taps a pen on her date pad.

"Who is that?" Lorene asks.

"He's the waiter that served you on Thursday, March ninth—the morning you had beverages at Coffee Call with Gloria Bolton."

I look at Lorene trying to picture the server in my mind.

"I don't think he was a regular," Lorene reports.

"Why is he important?" I inquire.

"He's deceased," Detective Chico tells us.

"Did he have blond hair and a goatee?" I seem to recall. "He couldn't have been more than twenty, poor thing. Was it Covid?"

"No," Chico replies. "His death was a homicide."

"That means he was murdered," Lorene qualifies.

I hardly know how to react to the news. "I'm so sorry," I say.

"As far as we can discern, Mr. Mason has no roots in Colombia, no family we can locate. He's still at the morgue in cold storage."

Lordy, I would hate for the county to keep my dead body frozen because nobody cared enough about me to bury or burn me. I think of the freedom Arthur must have experienced when his ashes were released over our cow pasture. I know he's with Jesus in Heaven now.

"What has any of that got to do with us?" Lorene asks.

"The M.E. called and told me you were coming over," Chico says.

That's not a crime, I think to myself.

"Murder is a crime, Mrs. Powell," she remarks as if having read my mind. I don't like this woman. She's far too smart and curt.

"You are making us very nervous, Detective Chico." I note that Lorene is trembling so bad I can hear her metal chair creaking. "Please, just ask your questions or tell us how we can help you."

The detective actually smiles.

I don't know how to react.

"Relax, ladies. I don't believe either of you are guilty of anything criminal," she tells us. "The results of Gloria Bolton's autopsy revealed she ingested a substance that causes blood clots."

"Blood clots!" Lorene and I simultaneously exclaim.

"Dorothy switched cups!" Lorene blurts out. "Somebody tried to kill her!" The chair under her buns tips over as she stands up.

* * *

After asking Dorothy Powell a few more questions, Detective Chico dismissed the ladies and decided to drive over to Captain Marilyn Colbert's office and deliver the critical news that has just been dumped on her by Lorene Perkins. Dorothy Powell's best friend has accused her of murder. "I'll be out for a lunch break," she tells Blake.

"You have a three o'clock with Channel 5," he reminds her.

"I should be back by then."

It is a clear spring day, warming up into the high sixties. Galena enjoys Tennessee weather more than what Miami, Florida offers on a daily basis, humid heat. It's nice experiencing seasonal changes.

The big drawback to accepting this job was leaving behind her family. And there was a Miami policeman she'd been dating. Long distance relationships have never worked too well for her. And filling the position of a hometown detective was never easy for the best of law officers. Continually, people phoned and asked to speak to Detective Lloyd Peters. Finally, Blake recorded a response to their requests, revealing he was deceased. It saved some office time.

Galena sometimes listened to the caller's remarks and heard the sadness in their voices. Do doubt, Detective Butch would be missed.

Then there was Ellie, his secretary and bride-to-be. She'd purchased Dorothy Powell's farm and returned to Columbia in February with her parents. Sometimes, she was outside the building in the parking lot gazing up at the second story. What a sad sight!

Last year, it was as if Evil had visited the fair southern town.

The Columbia Police Department is located on 707 North Main Street. The Chief of Police, Assistant Chief, and Captain of Investigations has offices in the building. Galena had not called ahead to schedule a meeting with the captain. Her news is urgent.

Galena burps the remnants of a chicken sandwich as she enters the building through double doors that have electronic surveillance to detect weapons. She leaves her gun at the front desk under lock and key. "Tell Captain Colbert I'm here to see her," she tells Jim.

The officer has already asked Galena for a date, so he is pleased to smooth the way for her visit. "Lookin' mighty fine, Detective."

When he winks, Galena cringes but smiles back.

"I was hopin' we could go on a real date." He leans his head through the open sliding-glass window. "How 'bout Friday night?"

"My schedule is pretty tight, Jim. Might have to be coffee again," she qualifies. "I'll let you know before Friday."

With disappointment shadowing his rugged face, he calls up to Captain Marilyn Colbert's office. Galena listens to a one-sided conversation that ends with, "She ain't in, her secretary says."

"Is that so?" Galena quirks her head to one side and makes eye contact with Jim. "Mind checking to see if she's signed out."

Jim thumbs through a six-by-nine, wire-bound book, and finds today's date. Every three months the info is plugged into a computer.

"Nope. Says she's still here," he reports to Galena.

"I'll just go on up and knock on her office door."

Jim grins, two crooked teeth showing. "Don't forgit to call me."

"I won't."

Galena steps lightly down the hall. Men in this town are chasing her like she's a hooker. Be damned if any of them will catch her in a dark corner at night. No one likes looking down the barrel of a .45—which she carries 24/7, even sleeps with. After what happened to the detective she replaced, she vowed to take no unnecessary chances.

Captain Colbert's door stands open, so Galena walks in. "Good afternoon, Penny. I need to see Captain Colbert. It's urgent."

Penny stops typing on her computer and checks her calendar.

"No appointment, tell the Captain I'm here," Galena spouts.

Penny cows and calls Colbert on the landline, even though the door to the captain's private sanctuary is shut. She glances at Galena.

"Detective Chico is here to see you," Penny announces.

Seconds later, the door to Colbert's office opens and a woman as black as a moonless night sky stands in the opening.

"Did I forget an appointment?" she queries with surprise.

"No." Galena approaches. "I have an update on the Gloria Bolton's murder case. Can we speak privately in your office?"

Penny watches the two women a moment then returns to her computer work. No need to tell her to hold calls, it's protocol.

Marilyn motions Galena to a chair in front of her desk.

"Thank you, I'll stand. What I have to say won't take long."

"Have you had lunch?" Marilyn removes a sandwich from her desk drawer. "I haven't, so tell me while I eat before I faint."

Galena inhales deeply and sits down. She waits a few minutes while Marilyn devours half of her sandwich then fills a mug from the coffee carafe sitting on the credenza behind her desk.

Marilyn swipes her mouth with a paper napkin and points at Galena. "Okay, Detective, tell me what you've got that's so urgent."

"I had a visit from Dorothy Powell and Lorene Perkins today."

"Coffee?" Marilyn sips from her mug.

"No, thanks." Galena waits a beat. "They didn't know the young guy that served their beverages at Coffee Call the Thursday Gloria Bolton ingested a lethal latte. I told them the server was dead. I also told them his death was a homicide. I wanted to see their reaction."

"Maybe you shouldn't have," Marilyn says. "Dorothy's an amateur detective. She fancies herself as a Nancy-Drew solving crimes."

"I don't think the women were intentionally involved, but Lorene blurted out that Dorothy switched coffee cups with Gloria Bolton that morning." Galena pauses for the news to be digested by Marilyn.

"Do I need to probe further?" Galena asks.

Marilyn abandons her desk and rolls her shoulders.

"Dorothy Powell is what? Eighty-two. Would she turn into an assassin at this late stage in her life?" Marilyn paces. "I doubt it."

"I don't believe her switching cups was intentional," Galena says. "But the woman has been through a lot since her husband Arthur was murdered two years ago. Kidnapped twice by an assassin that works for the Russian Mafia. That changes a person."

"I know you've read Mark Hagen's file. He murdered four of our citizens and was sent to prison for life. The CIA arranged his escape and used Dorothy as bait to capture Mafia bosses in four states. And I hear the guy they sent in to watch over Dorothy was sweet on her."

Surprised, Galena's mouth falls open. "That wasn't in the file."

"Clint Howard was CIA Agent Thomas Kessler's alias. He volunteered to move to Columbia and keep an eye on Mrs. Powell."

Why? was written all over Galena's face.

"I was told Dorothy resembled Kessler's deceased wife, though she's a good fifteen years older than him." Marilyn shakes her head.

"That sounds like the makings of a romance novel," Galena says.

Marilyn scrubs her tired eyes. Galena wants to caution her to get more sleep, but that isn't her place. The job always takes precedence over personal comfort. Didn't she know that from experience?

Sometimes finding out the hard away, law-enforcement people lose out on great relationships. Galena's engagement four years ago had failed because of the job. And now she is married to her work.

Probably, forever. "What do you want me to do about Mrs. Powell?"

"Get her in and give her a lie-detector test," Marilyn decides.

"What if she refuses?"

"We can get a court order, but I believe she will cooperate."

"Will do." Galena stands up. "I'll be in touch."

"You do that." Marilyn limps to the door and opens it. "Have a good rest of the afternoon, Detective Chico. Stay safe."

"Always."

5

WE HAVE BEEN BACK at Lorene's house since mid-afternoon. The May weather is refreshing, much warmer than April with its spring showers. I am seated in the swing on her back porch gazing at the small green heads of plants we put in the ground in March, which prompts me to think of Coffee Call's employee dying a few days after Gloria.

His death was too close to hers to be a coincidence.

"Are you mad at me?" Lorene asks as she sits with me.

"No, a little peeved," I reply. "It was my place to tell Detective Chico I switched cups with Gloria. I had good reason. She didn't like the taste of her blend. I was actually trying to be kind to the woman."

"Well, you can be grateful I didn't tell her how much you disliked her. How you were rivals in high school. And that she dated your Arthur before you did." Lorene looks at me. "I was kind to you."

I cannot help but laugh.

"This is not funny, Dorothy. Some people might think you slipped something in that coffee before you switched cups with Gloria."

"I'm not worried, Lorene. Folks in this town know me."

"People thought they knew that guy Ted somebody."

My feet hit the wood floor as the swing ceases to drift. "I'm not a serial killer, Lorene! How can you compare me to Ted Bundy?"

"Just saying . . ." Lorene stares into space.

I get up and walk to the back door.

"Where are you going, Dorothy?"

I turn around. "To Claire's. Where people trust me."

"Please don't! I'm so sorry. We can have pizza tonight and watch a movie together! I don't want to be alone. Please, Dorothy!"

The oomph slides out like a rotten banana run over by a bicycle.

"Okay, on one condition."

"What?" Lorene barters.

"No more talk about Gloria Bolton or death. Are we clear?"

"As a bell!"

We both hear the front door chimes go off. I wonder if this is a bad omen. "I should see who's come for a visit," Lorene says.

I limp over to the swing again, feeling a creaking in my bones as I sit down. Truth be told, I am worried about what people will think if they find out I switched cups with Gloria and she died because of the substance added to the coffee. I'm probably the only one worried the dose of death was intended for me since Gloria isn't the one breathing.

What a huge mess! Maybe my GG June is right. I am always getting into trouble. The backdoor opens and Lorene steps through.

"You have a visitor, Dorothy."

Who could it be? My daughter?

"Okay, I'm coming." I'm on the move again.

We enter the house together. Detective Chico stands in the foyer.

Surprise is on my face. I can't help but worry why she's come calling so soon after our visit to her office. "Am I under arrest?" I ask as the rug is pulled out from under me, literally, as I step closer.

I am losing balance and falling backward then hit the floor hard. The glittering lights around me are bright. They aren't real stars.

"Are you okay?" A face comes into focus, leaning over me. Then my eyes finally sharpen and I can see Detective Chico clearly.

"Did I just faint?" I shakily sit up.

"No, the new rug slipped out from under your feet," Lorene says then helps me to my feet. "I'm so sorry. Are you hurt?"

"My pride," I reply, but my butt stings.

"Let's sit down somewhere so we can talk," Galena suggests.

"In my den." Lorene helps me limp to the sofa.

Detective Chico says, "I'm sorry I startled you, Mrs. Powell, you are not under arrest. But I want you to take a lie-detector test."

"Why?" I ask.

"To explain why you switched cups with Gloria Bolton on March ninth when you met her for refreshments at Coffee Call."

"I already told you why." *Hadn't I?*

"Captain Colbert wants it on the record."

I look at Lorene for support. *What should I do?*

"Do I have a choice?" I ask, wishing Thomas Kessler were here to advise me. I could call my attorney son-in-law Ted for clarity.

"Yes, but under a court order, you would not have a choice," Galena explains. "You can have a lawyer present if you want."

"I want."

"You have twenty-four hours to get your ducks in a row, Mrs. Powell. Call me before then, and we'll set an appointment for your lie-detector test. I'll text you the address where it will be given."

My ducks in a row? I have always had trouble with planning ahead. Whenever I was certain of what came next, it usually didn't. Circumstances changed into something entirely different. Like the night I cooked supper for Arthur and he didn't come home. His death changed me forever. I don't even think the same way. That's why I detest unknowns. And, like it or not, I have to tell Claire everything. She has no idea I am in any way involved with Gloria Bolton's death.

Some secrets cannot be kept. I recall June's question.

"GG, why does Mama say you're always getting into trouble?"

6

IT IS ALREADY DARK outside and time to lock up the office for the day and head on home, although the two-bedroom apartment Detective Chico rented is far from feeling like home. Galena is hungry and thirsty for a huge burger and jug of draft beer. The overkill of coffee throughout the day has left a bitter taste in her mouth.

Dr. Cynthia Perkins' autopsy report on Danny Mason had arrived by courier an hour ago. Her lab assistant Gordy had phoned to make sure it arrived. Dr. Gordon Mills, a qualified mortician, preferred not to be formally addressed. A strange bird, he was funny and super intelligent. No close friends, he mostly kept company with the dead.

Galena had stayed late at the office after her secretary Blake left. She'd reviewed the Medical Examiner's statement regarding Mason's premature death. In her mind, he'd been murdered. At age twenty-one, no health issues showed up during the autopsy. Hired as a server by Coffee Call's manager a week prior to Gloria Bolton's encounter with a dose of death in her drink, he'd suspiciously quit his job the next day.

Nothing surprising in the restaurant business. Low-end personnel commonly worked enough hours to apply for government assistance then quit. Danny never did. Nobody at Coffee Call had heard from the drifter since. Galena had informed the manager that he was found dead in his Nashville apartment. His heart simply quit beating.

Danny had no priors so he was not in any criminal federal system. There was no social security number for him. It was like he'd been invented for a week to perform the heinous duty of murder.

Clearly, someone smarter than Danny had intended for Dorothy Powell to receive the latte to die for. He simply delivered the gift.

Luckily, Dorothy switched lattes with Gloria Bolton. She could not have known she was killing Gloria. Still, her statement had to be taken for the record. Perhaps by then, another suspect would surface.

Galena walked into the outer office and checked the landline. Calls were on hold, but anything important would ring on her cell.

A Latte to Die For

* * *

I roll in Claire's driveway at six p.m. and shut off my BMW motor, deciding to leave my overnight case locked in the trunk. I actually don't feel at home anywhere now. I need my own space. But in the back of my mind, I want to make space in my life for Tom. Purchasing a condo in Brentwood feels so final, like it will be my last resting place before I see Arthur again. I long to . . . what? Travel? At my age?

I am definitely depressed. I don't want to be here. I did not phone ahead to tell my daughter I was coming back and not spending the night with Lorene. To my chagrin, I cancelled my consultation appointment tomorrow with Dr. Sharra to discuss a facelift procedure.

Who needs to look better while in jail?

My daughter opens the backdoor before I can knock.

"Mama, what are you doing out here?"

"Am I interrupting some kind of kinky sex?"

Ted appears behind Claire and chuckles. "I wish."

"Come in, Mama, supper is still warm in the kitchen."

"Did I say I was hungry?" I am in a foul mood. This day sucks. Nothing I planned has worked out. Fate has had me by the tail and swinging me every which direction. I want to cry out to the dark and tell it to swallow me. Let's get this life over with and start a new one.

"Don't be too loud, June fell asleep on the sofa," Ted warns.

I push past the happy sexless couple and enter the den. My precious great granddaughter looks like a sleeping angel. I wonder if she has wings tucked under the Afghan. I should have listened to the wise counsel of this child and realized her previous statement was a warning. *Watch out, GG! Trouble is coming your way.*

I shed my sweater on the back of the dining room chair and lay my weary head on the table. "Do you have Tylenol?"

"Are you sick, Mama?" Ted asks, and I love that he no longer calls me Dorothy but thinks of me as his real family.

I lift my head marginally. "Only of heart."

"Here." Claire hands me two pain meds. "What's wrong with your heart?" She hovers over me like I'm a child.

I sit up and sigh. My gaze skitters between the two of them.

"I don't want to talk about it!"

I miss Arthur. I'm homeless. Jane Murphy wants to kick me out of the Canasta game I've played for twenty years, and Thomas Kessler had broken my heart and, even worse, I may never see him again. Plus, I need to tell Claire the police suspect I killed Gloria Bolton.

"I think I'm going to throw up!" I run to the hall bathroom.

I am seated on the commode with my head resting in my hands, my elbows on my skinny knees when the bathroom door opens.

"Mama, can I get you something?"

"Yes, a new life. Much younger, please."

Claire slips inside the bathroom and closes the door. "Something is dreadfully wrong. Tell me." She glares at me like a mama bear.

Words cannot express my distress. "Give me a minute." I shew her out of the bathroom, stand, and splash cold water in my face.

The hall seems endless as I tread down it behind Claire. I spy Ted seated at the dining room table with his hands resting on its shiny wood surface. The food and tablecloth are gone. "Claire," Ted says.

"Mama is upset. She has something to tell us."

I sit down in the Captain's Chair at the end of the table. Claire and Ted flank me, their eyes glued to me like ants stuck to flypaper.

"I don't know where to start." I look at one then the other.

"Anywhere is fine, Mama." Ted grasps my right hand and I feel so welcome. It's like a warm wind blows through me. I can trust him.

"Okay . . . let me see." I go back to that day . . .

Lorene and I are running fifteen minutes late. Gloria Bolton is already seated at a table in Coffee Call, fiddling with her iPhone.

Gloria Lake had been the most popular girl in our high school and I suspect she's accumulated dozens of friends since moving back to Columbia. I don't want to be jealous of her easy charm, winning ways, and great beauty, but I can't help myself. She's a show-stopper.

"So sorry we're late," Lorene apologizes to Gloria and takes a seat at the laminated table for four. "Have you ordered yet?"

I fill a seat at the table, quiet as a mouse cornered by a huge cat as I glance around the room. I love this bistro. The original restaurant is located in the heart of the New Orleans' French Quarter not far from the meandering Mississippi River. Famous for its *café aulait* coffees, *beignets* and fried French pastries coated in powdered sugar, Columbia's version is housed in an antiquated building with high ceilings that once was utilized as a storage building for international products arriving by ship during the early 19th century. The bistro has atmosphere-plus as the strong odor of ground coffee beans permeate the atmosphere.

Gloria has yet to make eye contact with me. I know she doesn't like me, but she likes Lorene, so she puts up with me. I won't let her steal my best friend from me. No way, Hosea! I sober at the thought.

Lorene and Gloria stop talking as our server arrives.

"You're new, aren't you?" Lorene looks up at the handsome young guy. He winks at her, flirting to get a better tip, I'm betting.

"Girls, are you ready to order?" Gloria inquires.

She has taken charge of our get-together when Lorene was the one that arranged for us to meet here for coffee. I can only submit.

"Dorothy, what do you want?" Lorene worries I'm so quiet. She's hoping I'll mind my manners and not set Gloria off.

I am reminded that oil and water don't mix as I open the laminated menu. There are multiple choices of frozen coffee drinks listed since summer approaches. The restaurant will soon be hopping with teens on summer break. Adults will use the drive-through to avoid the frivolity. "A peppermint mocha," I decide. "Extra whip cream."

Lorene pats Gloria's hand. "My treat today, ladies."

"That's very nice of you, Lorene," I comment.

Our server shifts from one foot to the other, waiting for our order.

"I'll try the special printed in French," Gloria tells our server.

"Are you sure? It's quite a concoction," he warns.

"I like surprises." Gloria drops the menu.

"What is your name?" I ask the guy.

"Danny," he replies. "Our famous beignets are on special today." Gloria looks at Lorene for an opinion.

"Sounds good," I decide, "but I insist on paying the tab."

"An order is three beignets; would you like to double it?"

I glance up at Danny. "Sure!" I chuckle. "We're splurging today."

Lorene looks at me like I've lost my mind.

"I don't usually eat fattening foods," Gloria stoically remarks.

"If you did, what is your favorite pastry?" I inquire.

"Some kind with a creamy filling," she replies.

"What flavor?" Danny stands behind Gloria but stares at me.

"I once had an almond pastry in Baton Rouge."

"Are you from Louisiana?" he inquires.

"No, but I've traveled all over the world."

Lucky you! I think then say, "Bring Gloria two of those!"

A frown. "I really shouldn't." She pats her flat stomach.

"Isn't that overkill?" Lorene asks. "I thought we were having beignets. It's too much, Dorothy." She shakes her head at me.

Behave yourself, Dorothy. I admit I'm being naughty.

But I can see that temptation has taken hold of Gloria and won't let go. "What're a few calories among friends?" I ask them both.

"Well, put like that . . ." Gloria half chuckles.

Danny takes our order and disappears behind the counter. We spend the time waiting for our food and drinks to arrive by discussing the upcoming spring ball held at the Senior Citizen Center in late May.

"Gerry has hired a jazz band and the food will be catered by Troy's Seafood and Steak," Gloria says. "There's a small fee, of course."

"How much?" Lorene asks.

My good friend is always on a tighter budget than I am. I know she's invested the insurance money Crawford left her in the stock market and lives off her social security check. Her farm has no mortgage. She can afford to do anything she wants, but resists.

"Twenty-five dollars per person," Gloria replies. "Gerry will make sure everyone who wants to attend can—it's bank sponsored."

That's not a small fee in my estimation. I don't comment.

We make more small talk. In less than fifteen minutes, our lattes arrive in glistening white ceramic cups, alongside a double order of beignets and Gloria's two almond pastries. *Overkill,* like Lorene said.

The pastries and lattes smell divine since I skipped breakfast and planned ahead on splurging on sugar calories, making dadgum sure Gloria and Lorene did, too. If I'm going to gain weight, they will, too.

"Thank you, Danny," I tell him and hand him my credit card.
"No problem, Mrs. Powell." He grins then walks away.
Gloria leans over the table slightly. "Do you know him?"
"Who, Danny? No," I reply as I snap a paper napkin over my lap.
"Well, he seems to know you, Dorothy," Lorene interjects.
"He must have heard us talking." I explain the phenomenon.
"No, we've only used our first names," Gloria notes.
"Is it important?" I ask, a bit perturbed at the interrogation. . .

I stop talking and glare at my family. "I never realized Danny's knowing me was important at the time," I tell Claire.
"Go on, Mama, tell us more," Ted urges.

Gloria takes a sip of her French-named latte and frowns.
"What? You don't like it?" Lorene notes.
"It's too bitter," Gloria replies. "A lot of caffeine, I expect."
"Here, I'll switch with you." I slide my latte her way.
"No, it's okay. I'll dump it and order another," Gloria decides.
"No, don't do that," I insist. "I promise you'll like my Peppermint Mocha." I switch coffees, congratulating myself for a kind deed.
Danny returns with my card and I sign the tab, leaving him a healthy tip. We eat our pastries and part ways an hour later. . .

"What is it about this story that bothers you, Mama?"
The pertinent question comes from Ted.
"I learned from the detective that replaced Lloyd Peters that our server was murdered a few days after Lorene and I had coffee with Gloria at Coffee Call. Something in my latte caused Gloria's stroke."
Ted's eyes widen. "So, you were meant to have the latte to die for," he concludes. "The dose of death was meant for you."
"Apparently." Tears materialize in my gaze. "When I switched coffees with Gloria, I killed her." More tears drip down my cheeks.
"Oh, Mama!" Claire hugs me. "You could not have known."
I love my daughter; she's so reasonable. And she is right.

7

Tuesday, May 9

THE LIE-DETECTOR TEST is administered in Judge Katy Walker's courthouse office. Captain Marilyn Colbert, Detective Galena Chico, and my son-in-law Theodore Harold Burkes, III are present.

I've never taken a lie-detector test so everything feels strange as the officer performing the test attaches a mechanism to my body that will alert him if I am purposely lying when answering a question. I have no idea what questions he will ask me. It's not like I'm a politician.

"Now, Mama, don't be scared." Ted kneels beside me as I sit in a chair, feeling like it might be electric and soon I will see Arthur.

"Actually, I am a little nervous," I whisper in his ear.

"Mrs. Powell? We aren't trying to trick you, honestly."

I look up at Captain Colbert. "I appreciate that. I just want to get to the bottom of what happened to Gloria so justice will prevail."

Boy, am I a brave soul! I talk a good talk, but inside . . .

"My name is Floyd, Mrs. Powell. I will be asking you a series of questions. Please answer yes or no, unless I ask you to explain."

"Yes, sir." I am back in elementary school, fully obedient.

"First, we'll establish a line on my equipment, then we'll begin."

I nod. It's not a statement I understand, so I won't comment.

"What is your name?" Floyd asks me.

"Dorothy Jean Powell."

"When is your birthday?"

"June 25, 1939," I reply.

"You are eighty-two years old," he says.

"Yes." *Going on old*, I think to myself.

He asks the governor's name and a few other questions that are commonly known. I am proud to know all those answers.

"I think we're ready to proceed." He looks at Captain Colbert.

She takes a page of questions from Detective Chico and hands it to Floyd. My Ted is standing a few feet away in a corner, watching.

I know he will protect me if anyone tries to abuse my rights.

"Detective Chico, read Mrs. Powell's Miranda Rights," Floyd says.

I listen and agree to answer honestly the questions asked.

Forty-five minutes pass. The test is over and I'm actually sweating.

"You did real good, Mama," Ted tells me. "Let's go."

We exit the courthouse. "Do you think they believed me?"

"You passed the test, Mama, that's all they need."

I let go of a breath I've been holding for a while.

* * *

Marilyn Colbert switches off the recorder. "I don't think Mrs. Powell purposely tried to hurt Gloria Bolton when she switched coffees with her, do you?" She stares at Detective Chico.

"No, I don't. But it appears she feels guilty for Gloria's death."

"I know she does," Floyd remarks. "Every time the deceased's name was mentioned, Mrs. Powell's blood pressure shot up a notch."

Marilyn shakes her head. "I've never known an elderly woman that could get into so much trouble *accidentally*. She is a walking nightmare, a curse to herself that affects many around her. She has put her poor daughter Claire through hell in the past two years."

"I've read about the Crystal Creek murders. The story is the making of a novel, if one can believe that truth is more powerful than fiction," Galena comments. "So, Captain Colbert? What comes next?"

"I need to find out who hired Danny Mason to travel to Columbia, Tennessee, to murder Dorothy Powell," Marilyn replies. "I suspect the Russia Mafia is involved, but that has to be proven."

"Payback is a powerful motive," Floyd interjects.

"Maybe I should talk to someone at TBI," Galena suggests.

"Last fall, the CIA sent an agent to Columbia to keep an eye on Mrs. Powell after they arranged for Mark Hagen to escape a maximum-security prison outside of Knoxville, Tennessee," Marilyn recalls.

"Thomas Kessler, posing as Clint Howard," Galena recalls.

"A friend that graduated college with me works for the Tennessee Bureau of Investigations," Galena reveals. "I'll pick his brain."

"You do that," Marilyn says. "We're finished here today."

"I'll clean up and get out of Judge Walker's office," Floyd offers.

"Let's keep this information between us," Marilyn says. "I don't want the news media broadcasting anything useful to our enemies."

* * *

"Don't you want to come home with me?" Ted asks Dorothy.

"No, take me to Lorene's house." I know I will have a crying spell and don't want Claire to witness my semi-nervous breakdown.

"What about your car?" he asks.

"It will be fine parked outside the courthouse. I'll get Lorene to drive me back to fetch it." I am far too nervous to drive a vehicle.

"You're choice." Ted ignites his mercury-gray Mercedes Benz and flies down the street. I pray he isn't ticketed, but he doesn't seem worried. I want to ask him if he's cheating on my Claire. He's not a golden catch anymore—nor nearly as handsome as Thomas Kessler. In his mid-fifties, his light-brown hair is thinning in the crown and he's put on extra weight around his torso. He drinks too much alcohol and doesn't exercise regularly. I fear that's a recipe for a heart attack.

But I won't grill him today; he's been super nice to me.

"You're mighty quiet, Mama."

"Just lost in my thoughts, Theodore."

"You answered well today. Off the hook for Gloria's death."

I glare at him as he drives over the speed limit toward Lorene's house. "Do you think whoever sent Danny will send someone else?"

"To murder you? No," Ted replies.

"I think someone in the Russian Mafia is pissed off at me. I don't think they will be satisfied until I'm off this planet," I predict.

"Do you want me to hire a private detective?"

This is a novel idea. "Someone to track down the people that hired Danny to murder me?" I feel a bit excited about the prospect.

"Yes, I know plenty of hungry PIs in Nashville. It's not like you don't have the money, now that you've sold your farm."

"Let me think about it, Ted."

"Sure."

We drive another fifteen minutes. He rolls off the main highway and up Lorene's ascending gravel driveway. She's out in the front yard watering her budding plants. I see confusion in her expression.

"Did you bring your overnight case?" Ted asks me.

"No need, half my things are still at Lorene's."

"What do you want me to tell Claire?"

"Tell her I'll be back in a few days," I reply. "I need to figure out a few things first, Ted. Mainly, whether I want a Private Eye following me around. Claire can't know. She asks too many questions."

He chuckles as I get out of the car. "Thanks, Ted."

"No problem, Mama." He makes the circle and drives away.

Lorene walks over to me, her hands wet with dirt. "Did you tell me you were coming back today?"

"No, but I'm home, honey." I tromp past her and go inside the house, my tears so heavy I can hardly wait to release them.

Actually, I let out a huge scream. The release is so remarkable I do it again and again and again. Thank God, Claire is not here.

My cell phone vibrates in my purse. I look at the caller.

Lorene stands by my side. "What was all that screaming about?"

It's Dr. Sharra's office. "I have to take this, Lorene." I step out the back door onto the porch and close it for privacy. What a day!

8

IT'S ALREADY 4:45 P.M. on Tuesday when I'm seated in the office of Dr. Lyle Sharra. Don't ask me why, but somehow treating myself to a facelift procedure counteracts my hysteria about being hunted down by yet another serial killer. I feel the onset of old-age depression creeping over me. I want to look younger, if not for Tom, for myself.

Ginger, Dr. Sharra's assistant, has taken separate x-rays of the inner workings of my face. The results are on the screen in front of me. I look like an alien from outer space, but I'm gaining an appreciation for the human body's muscle and skeletal network underneath my skin. God has uniquely designed each of us.

A bit nervous. I pray Dr. Sharra is competent in his profession.

I've seen people on TV with their skin and muscles so tight around their mouths they look weird. I have droopy eyelids, so that is why my insurance is paying for part of the surgery. The packet of information in front of me describes a complete overhaul of the face.

All wrinkles and sags removed. I've opted for that image.

"Mrs. Powell, I'm so pleased you've decided to move forward."

Dr. Sharra speaks with a German accent, but his resume is impressive and his charge for the procedure is not cost-prohibitive.

"How do you feel today?" he inquires.

"I've had quite a day, Dr. Sharra." I won't go into details.

"Well, all is well that turns out well, right?" he stoically remarks. "Have you reviewed the cost of our deluxe package?"

"I have." Compared to many Tennesseans, I am a wealthy woman for the daughter of a Methodist minister who is retired from public-school teaching and the widow of a farmer. I still have more than half of the half-million-dollar insurance policy payout from Arthur's death. Plus, Ellie Simpson paid me $895,000 for my house on 200 acres.

"Good, good," he says with a white dental-teeth smile.

"By the way, who cancelled their appointment?" I'm curious.

"Gloria Ann Bolton," he replies.

"But she died two months ago." I am shocked.

"No one cancelled her appointment," he explains. "It was an oversight, so I had Ginger call you. Is that a problem?"

I think karma is playing a trick on me. Of all people, I despise the idea of taking Gloria's appointment slot. It seems cruelly unfair.

"Look . . ." Dr. Sharra expels a breath, "I know you were friends with Mrs. Bolton. If you don't want to do this today, we'll reschedule."

"No." I look at him, tears in my eyes. I want to confess that I gave Gloria the coffee laced with a substance that killed her. But I won't.

"Okay, if you're sure, let's proceed."

He points out the areas of my face where I've lost muscle mass and makes suggestions where to nip and tuck. I'll have temporary scars but they will eventually fade, and makeup does wonders to cover up.

We set up a time for the surgery: Friday, June second.

* * *

I'm back at Lorene's house by six fifteen with a large container of Kentucky Fried Chicken with all the trimmings for two people. I place our supper on the breakfast bar and park my carcass in a barstool.

"Well, are you going to have the surgery?" Lorene asks as she pours sugar-sweet decaf tea over ice cubes into two tall tumblers.

"Friday morning, June second," I reply.

"That's only three weeks away; have you told Claire?"

"No, only you. I don't want my family to know."

"Why not, is it going to cost you a pretty penny?"

"My insurance covers part of the surgery—droopy eyelids, and I've opted to take the deluxe package." I won't divulge the total cost.

"Doesn't matter, you can afford it, friend. And you deserve it."

I reach across the bar to grasp her hand. "I don't deserve a friend as sweet and considerate as you are, Lorene. You are like the sister I never had." She is aware my only brother is deceased. Arthur and my son Lance are in Heaven now, so friendships are dear to me.

"I'll say the blessing over our food," Lorene volunteers as she spies tears gathering in my eyes. I nod, bow my head, and sniffle.

"Dear Heavenly Father: You have given me and Dorothy a good, long life. We are so thankful for our family and friends. We pray you will bless this food to the nourishment of our bodies. Amen."

"Amen," I add and rip into our container of food.

* * *

"You're working late again," Claire chides Ted as he comes through the backdoor. It's already well after ten p.m. She is in the kitchen stirring dough that will turn into chocolate-chip cookies for Billy's kindergarten class tomorrow. It's his turn to bring treats on Wednesday. Helen, Claire's daughter and Billy's mother, was recently hired by an advertisement firm as a sales rep. She also worked late tonight so Billy spent the night—already in the bed, thank goodness.

"Work—the nature of the beast," Ted says regarding the job.

"How did the lie-detector test go for Mama?" she asks.

"Passed with flying colors."

"I expected you home for supper." Claire glances his way.

"Something came up at the office." Ted pecks his wife on the cheek. "Sorry, I should have called." He sniffs the air. "Something smells mighty tempting. Cookies?" He sheds his jacket.

"Yes, but not for you, my Jolly Good Elf. I put you on a diet, or did you forget? We had baked cod with slaw and broccoli for supper tonight." Claire pats out the cookies on a greased baking sheet.

"I grabbed a sandwich earlier." Ted racks his jacket in the foyer closet. "You are a cruel woman, Claire Burkes. You keep me on the straight and narrow." He hopes the conversation won't go south.

"I sincerely hope so." Claire had found pink lipstick on the collar of his white shirt this past Saturday—not the first time, either.

"You *hope* so? What does that mean?"

His forehead furrows.

"Are you cheating on me with another woman, Ted?"

He bursts out laughing. "Where did that come from, Claire?"

"Why was their lipstick on your white shirt from last Friday's dinner out with that new country-western singer? Kelly somebody."

Ted approaches Claire and places his hands on her shoulders. "I did give her a hug when we parted, but that's not sexual contact."

Claire bit her lip, dropping the wooden spoon on the bar.

"I'm telling you the truth, honey. I love you. I'm not cheating."

Claire inhales deeply, looks him in the eye, to evaluate the attorney's sincerity. He's lied before, about insignificant things—like eating dessert when he took clients out to dinner. This was different.

"Okay, I believe you." Claire picks up her spoon and points it at him like a weapon. "But, if I ever catch you lying about seeing another woman, I will personally punch out your lights! Are we clear?"

Stunned, words evade him. *Murder?*

"Granny, whose lights are you gonna punch out?" Billy asks as he stumbles into the den, scrubbing sleepy bugs from his eyes.

"It's just a saying, son. No one's lights are going out."

"Why are you up, Billy?" Claire asks.

"I saw a buggerman, Granny."

"No buggermen in our house, son." Ted gathers Billy in his arms and threads his thick fingers through the boy's tangled dark hair.

"Will you put him back to bed?" Claire looks at Ted.

"Sure. Then I'm taking a shower and hitting the sack."

"I'll be to bed soon." Something nags at Claire's psyche. Ted is not being entirely honest with her about what he does after normal work hours. As of late, he's been distant in bed. She understands him well enough to know he's not old enough to sexually fizzle out.

So, who has grabbed his attention?

9

"YOU NEVER SAID HOW the lie-detector test went," Lorene says as she cuts off the Channel 5 news on the television at 10:30 p.m.

"Can we talk about it tomorrow?" I yawn, tired from the long day.

"I don't think I can sleep well if I don't know," Lorene says.

"Okay, but you only get the abbreviated version," I decide and explain what happened in general. "Everyone was nice to me."

"But did they believe you didn't switch coffees on purpose?"

"I did switch coffees on purpose, and I told Floyd that."

"I'm proud of you for admitting the truth, Dorothy," Lorene says. "When you finished, did you see the printout of your responses?"

"No," I reply. "Is that important?"

"I don't know, is it?" Lorene looks concerned.

I clamp my lips, no longer sleepy. "Is this an interrogation? Do you think I purposely tried to hurt Gloria?" Whose side is Lorene on?

"Of course not, I'm just pointing out the obvious."

"And what is the obvious?" I ask.

"They probably don't know how much you disliked Gloria."

"Well, I sure didn't tell them that!"

"Did they ask you about your prior relationship with her?"

Lorene is bent on destroying my rest tonight, and I'm ready to slap her. "I told them we were friends." I'm sticking to my story.

"Okay, point in reference, how did you react on paper when asked that question?" Lorene glares at me. "Just saying, are you in trouble?"

I frown. "I wasn't, until you pointed out I might be."

She has no comment.

"I'm going up to bed." Not that I plan to sleep anytime soon.

"I'm sorry if I upset you, Dorothy."

"You didn't," I lie and trot up the stairs to the guest bedroom on the second floor. I put on my PJs, brush my teeth, read a Psalm in the King James Bible, and try to recall how the lie-detector test came off.

The Lord's Prayer does not put me at ease. God is in Heaven, and I have to deal with murder on earth. I roll one way in the queen bed, then the other; I cannot settle down to sleep. I'm a nervous wreck.

And it's your fault, Lorene. I think our friendship is ruined.

It's close to midnight when I phone my son-in-law Ted.

"Yeah?" he sleepily answers.

"This is Mama—uh, Dorothy, Theodore."

"Mama!"

I can hear the hysteria in his voice.

"Are you okay? Did something bad happen?"

"I don't know, Ted. Did Floyd show you the printout of my responses to the questions he asked me this morning?"

"The lie-detector test? No."

"I passed it, didn't I?"

"I think so," Ted replies.

"*Think* is not a comforting answer."

"If you had failed the test, they would've told me, I'm your lawyer," Ted says, fully awake and perturbed at the interrupted sleep.

"Would you contact Captain Colbert tomorrow and ask to see my responses, Ted? I need to know if, well, if I said something amiss."

"Like what?"

"I don't know, that's why I want you to check."

"Look, Dorothy . . ."

I'm no longer Mama and that tells me he's upset with my call during the middle of the night.

"Look, how?" Let's qualify that statement.

"Did you suggest to Claire that I might be having an affair?"

This question comes out of nowhere.

"Did you, Dorothy?"

I think about my answer before speaking.

"Did something happen I should know about?" I inquire.

"Nothing that is any of your business, Dorothy."

"Are you mad at me, Theodore? Because if you are, I can hire another attorney to represent me to the Columbia Police Department."

"Why don't you do that, Dorothy! Good night!"

I sit up in bed and stare at my silent cell phone. Ted hates me. I no longer have a lawyer. Lorene thinks I said something incriminating that will suggest I purposely killed Gloria Bolton. And I can't sleep.

I get out of bed and go downstairs to fume over my situation.

Already Wednesday, it's after two a.m., and I have read several additional passages of Psalm from the King James Bible. I've prayed Arthur will somehow tell me what he thinks I should do. I don't want to hire another lawyer, but my son-in-law is furious with me. He knows I've expressed my opinion to Claire about the lipstick she found on his shirt collar. Lawyers have a sixth sense about these things.

If Claire finds out Ted and I had words, she'll be mad at me, too. I hear creaking floors, and glance up to see Lorene standing there.

"I heard noises," she says. "How long have you been up?"

"I never went to sleep, Lorene. I'm in trouble."

"With the law?"

"No, with my son-in-law."

"Theodore?" Lorene perches on the arm of the sofa since Crawford's recliner is occupied by me. "I thought he represented you during the lie-detector test." She yawns and scrubs her sleepy eyelids.

"I messed up and phoned him."

"Tonight? Why?"

"To ask him if he saw the results of my lie-detector test," I reply. "He hasn't. I made him mad by waking him up. Then he accuses me of suggesting he's cheating on Claire. I have to hire another attorney."

"Dorothy Powell! How can you get into so much trouble?"

"That's what GG thinks—that's my Great Granddaughter," I decode. "June is wiser than all the rest of us put together."

At that comment, Lorene bursts out laughing.

Me? I bawl and pray for Jesus to help me out of my jam.

Lorene only continues to snicker. Such are friends!

10

Wednesday, May 10

I AM BACK AT BURKES' house in Brentwood by ten a.m. I have a key, so I let myself in. I wonder if Ted told her about our conversation last night. The note on the bar is for me—in case I come home—she's at Billy's school serving cookies to his second-grade class. I toss my purse on the bar and collapse in a barstool, worried over life's issues.

I somehow must mend my relationship with Ted. However, I suspect he has a guilty conscious or would not have to quickly accused me of interfering with his marriage. I wonder if Ted and Claire had a fight before I spoke to him on the phone last night.

What had prompted his outburst?

Is he cheating on Claire?

I find biscuits wrapped in tinfoil in the oven. The butter dish is on the counter, mushy from oven heat and perfect to slather on a biscuit microwaved for fifteen seconds. Add jelly and it's a feast.

At 4 a.m. this morning, I had finally fallen asleep on Lorene's sofa. When I woke up at eight, she was already gone. A hair appointment.

I'd left her a scribbled note on the breakfast bar that I was returning to Claire's to straighten out things with Ted. Hopefully, by now, he would have realized I wasn't myself last night.

I never intended to hurt Claire or Ted.

The Burkes' house feels like a good home. It is cozy and inviting and I'm glad to be alone to plot my day. As I walk through the den, I note the embers simmering in the den's fireplace. The odors from breakfast linger. I patter down the hall and enter the guest bedroom.

As I lay in bed, I contemplate renting an apartment or condo. Claire and Ted need their space. My comments regarding their strained marriage will only create more strife between them. I despise the D word. And that isn't Double D-D, it stands for "divorce."

The rift with Ted is my fault. We should not end up enemies instead of in-laws. God, help us! I feel like a good healthy cry.

I hear the backdoor open and sit up in bed. Footfalls in the hallway reach my ears. Claire appears in the doorway.

"Mama, when did you get here?"

"An hour or so ago." I crawl slowly out of bed.

"I need to put away the groceries. Want some coffee?"

"Sure." I trail her down the hall through the den to the kitchen.

Two paper sacks of groceries are parked on the breakfast bar.

"I need to tell you something, Claire."

"Tell me what?" She starts putting the groceries away.

"About what Ted and I said to each other last night," I reply.

"Oh. That late phone call last night—was that you?"

I nod, denying tears. "It was a misunderstanding. I love Ted."

"Whatever was said, I'm sure he's already forgotten it."

"I don't think so," I counter.

"Mama, it's a mother-in-law/son-in-law thing." She blows off my comment. "When he gets home tonight, you'll make amends."

I shake my head. "He resigned as my lawyer."

Claire takes my hand. "Okay, tell me exactly what was said during that phone call last night." She escorts me to the sofa. "Sit down."

"I was upset when I called him," I explain. "Can we have coffee first?" I feel the need of a plug of caffeine to bolster my confidence.

"Sure." Claire stirs around in the kitchen and gets the coffeemaker in gear to do its thing. "Now, tell me everything, Mama."

I feel like a sheep being led to the slaughter. I'm at fault, not Ted. I sigh.

"Mama, I'm on your side."

"That's what Lorene says, but she keeps asking me questions about how I responded to the lie-detector test yesterday morning." I clasp my hands on the bar and notice how badly I need a manicure.

"What kind of questions?" Claire leans over the bar.

"Did I see the printed results? Did I react improperly to any of the questions? Did the police believe I told the truth?"

"You know what you said, Mama. Why does it upset you?"

"Well, I said Gloria and I were friends," I reply. "That is a lie; I don't like the woman. I want to know if my lie showed up on the test?"

"It's a little thing, Mama. Women get those feelings."

"Well, I phoned Ted because I couldn't sleep to ask him if Floyd showed him the printed results of my interview," I explain.

"Who's Floyd?"

"The officer that gave me the test," I explain. "Did he?"

Claire shakes her head. "He never talked to me about that."

"So . . . while we were talking, he accused me of meddling in your marriage. Did you two have a fuss yesterday?" Now, I'm meddling.

"Mama, that's between me and Ted." Claire frowns.

"Just tell me if you did, I don't need to know the details."

She nods, tears in her robin-blue eyes. "I found pink lipstick on his shirt collar this past Saturday. He denied cheating on me, and I want to believe him." Her lips are trembling.

"But you don't." I nod. It's worse than I thought. "I'm moving to my own place as soon as possible. Three's a crowd in this house."

"Are you sure?"

"Yes, I'm contacting a real-estate agent this afternoon to make arrangements to view properties this week." I'm not sure I will have the time. My standing hair appointment is tomorrow in Columbia. And I can't on Friday since I'm playing Canasta with my friends at the Senior Citizen Center. I refuse to let Jane Murphy kick me out and replace me with her friend. That leaves only Saturday as a possibility.

Unless I call a realtor today and look this afternoon.

"Well, as long as you are close by, I'm fine with it."

Claire wants me out of her hair as bad as Theodore does. I might move back to Columbia and rent an apartment in the same senior-citizen complex where Alicia Colby lives. This is not a good time to tell Claire I have set a date to have cosmetic surgery. I sober at the idea.

"What do you want for lunch, Mama?"

"Nothing, thanks. Please apologize to Ted for my bad behavior last night," I say then gather my purse and jacket.

"Mama? You don't have to leave."

"I know. I just don't feel at home anywhere these days."

"I'm so sorry. You are always welcome here."

"Thank you." I reach out for Claire's hand.

She smiles sweetly and squeezes it.

I try not to be sad, but I am thinking of Thomas Kessler. If he were here, I could lean on him. Even cry on his shoulder. I want to feel loved again, to have my own home—or is it too late?

Our silence is too uncomfortable.

"If you intend to view properties this afternoon, you should call an agency and request an agent to show you around," Claire says.

I ponder my possibilities.

"Not today. Maybe on Saturday," I decide.

Claire nods, but she is not smiling. She wants me settled in my own place as much as Ted does. I am a fifth wheel on a marriage wagon that's struggling to go forward. I am not helping matters.

"I love you, daughter of mine," I say.

"I love you, mother of mine."

We hug before I leave yet again. I'm always going and going and going and never staying. Maybe I should not have sold my home.

11

THE SENIOR LIVING COMPLEX is located on the south side of Columbia. It is spanking-new, a red brick with a Kelly-green tin roof. Flowerbeds are nestled around the huge front porch featuring multiple rocking chairs where the elderly can sit, converse, and enjoy the outdoor view as seasons come and go. Miss Alicia Anderton Colby occupies one of those rockers as I approach the porch.

"Well, well," she says, "look what the cats dragged up."

I pause to glare at my elderly English friend—not that I'm that much younger. "Did I miss something? Are you peeved at me, Alicia?"

She cracks a smile as her bones crunch when she stands—at least in my imagination. "Just practicing some common American quips."

I laugh. "Well, I'm glad I'm not in the doghouse." I hug her. She is tall and slender, but shorter than I am. "You haven't heard of that old saying?" I inquire. "It just means I'm not in any trouble."

"No, at least not with me." Alicia has trouble standing.

I grasp her arm. "Are you getting enough exercise in this place?" I am concerned that her physical strength may be waning.

"I go to an exercise-therapy class twice a week," Alicia says, grasping my arm hard as we enter the vaulted foyer of the complex.

"Show me your room," I tell her as we walk.

Guests are milling around the glass-topped atrium, a few signing the register to check out their relatives for a trip outside the facility.

We go down a short hall and take the elevator up to the second floor. The number for Alicia's independent one-bedroom apartment is on a metal plate attached to the door next to a call button.

"Here we are, Dorothy." She waves her right hand over a key panel and the door clicks open. "Prepped for wheelchair entrance."

"Sweet!" I say as Alicia turns around to stare at me.

"I haven't heard that expression before," she comments.

"My grandson Benjamin, it's his pick," I explain. "It means great." I glance around the compact living-kitchen combo.

Alicia is frowning.

"I know, sweet really doesn't make sense, but what in life does?"

"What famous person said that?"

"Someone above my paygrade." I am full of quotes today.

Alicia points to a door. "This way to my bedroom."

We enter an ample-sized bedroom and walk straight into a full bathroom featuring a walk-in bathtub/shower unit.

"This is great, Alicia!" I hail her choice for apartment living. "Are units like these very expensive?" I ask, still hoping to travel overseas.

"Not cheap, but the price should not bother you."

Everyone thinks I'm rich, but the dollar doesn't go as far as it used to. I trail Alicia back into the living area and take a seat on the sofa.

"The furniture is yours, right?" I pat the plush cushion seat.

"Yes, I sold some of my things but I'm comfortable here."

I place my hands on my bony knees. "I'm thinking of renting one of these apartments for myself. I can't keep running from Claire's to Lorene's in order to have a roof over my head. Besides, Lorene mentioned that Graham and Cynthia wanted to move in with her."

"Oh, really?" Alicia's gaze widens.

"What? Does that surprise you?" I ask.

"Did Lorene give you the details behind the request?"

"No, and I didn't pry."

"You're inferring I did," Alicia reacted.

"No, dear . . . I didn't mean that at all. What details?"

"Lorene doesn't want it getting around."

"What getting around?" I am now bent on discovery.

"You won't tell Claire or the girls at the Senior Citizen Center if I tell you?" Alicia acts as if Lorene's secret belongs to the CIA.

I heave a sigh. "If you promised Lorene not to tell anyone, don't tell me. I don't want to cause any trouble between you two."

Alicia's thin lips fold into her clamped mouth as she considers my comment. She's dying to tell me, but won't betray a friend.

"Let's talk about something else," I suggest. "Do you have summer plans? A trip to Europe maybe to visit old friends?"

"All my old friends are dead, Dorothy."

"You could take a cruise in the Caribbean," I suggest.

"I might, would you go with me?"

"It depends on when you book the trip," I reply. "It's sort of a secret, but I am having some cosmetic work done in early June. I'll need to heal before I leave town. My daughter doesn't know."

"My lips are sealed," Alicia assures me with another metaphor.

Silence suggests that we've run out of topics to discuss.

"Well, I should go, Alicia. It's been wonderful seeing you again," I tell her. "Anytime you want to have lunch at the Senior Citizen Center, just call either me or Lorene and one of us will fetch you."

Alicia tries to stands and falls back in her recliner.

"Don't get up, dear, I know my way out."

"Thank you for coming by to see me, Dorothy."

I lean over and hug her. "Call if I can help you in any way. You are a good friend and I will always hold you dear in my heart."

The door is closed between me and the transplanted English woman. I feel our time for camaraderie has passed. It makes me feel sad. But I still wonder what secret Lorene is keeping from me.

Instead of stopping at Lorene's house, I pass her driveway and continue on a few miles. My car knows its way home as I turn right into the gravel driveway that formerly belonged to me. The early twentieth-century farmhouse looms in the distance. Set high on a hill, its exterior white siding almost glistens in the noonday sunlight.

The terrain surrounding the house is a far contrast to winter's storehouse when I sold the house to Ellie. Today, the budding trees are a trajectory of constant green. The sky is a deep blue, and the sun is a diamond stuck in the middle. A white-picket fence has been added to the right side halfway up the driveway. Radiant red tulips march in a line alongside the fence that ends before the driveway curves in front of the house. I park under an oak tree in the circle driveway.

I exit my BMW and just stand there. So many memories slip through my scattered thoughts. Then I focus on the moment.

I'm thinking of trading my car for a pickup truck—like the one Arthur drove. I don't need to be uppity just because I have money.

And a Ford truck gets good mileage. Lord knows I drive enough miles between Columbia and Nashville.

Am I getting closer to buying my own place, too?

I know, I told Alicia I might move into the new senior complex but I don't actually feel old—yet I am. Wasteful thought.

Like my mother used to say, "Whatever age you are, you still feel like you're seventeen." Actually, birthdays seem irrelevant until they come around once a year. I will be eighty-three this June 25.

Ellie walks around the house and waves. "I thought I heard a car drive up." She approaches me with a radiant smile on her pretty face.

"I hope I'm not interrupting anything important," I say. "I had a hankering to see the house again." I had not been inside since the day we did a walk-through before Ellie signed the closing papers.

"Come in and have a cold glass of tea with me," Ellie says. "I've been planting a garden out back." She walks toward the front porch.

"Seems like we're going to have a hot summer," I forecast as I trail behind her a few steps. "But today is perfect."

"Global warming—both in summer and winter." She laughs.

"Blame the weather on people—ask me, God is in control."

"I fully agree." Ellie opens the front door for us.

I step into the foyer and look up the stairs. I know exactly where the bedrooms are. I follow Ellie past the dining room. Except for the furniture, the interior of my former updated house looks the same.

As we enter the breakfast room, the odor of vegetable soup simmering on the stove permeates the atmosphere. The large round breakfast table is mine; a gift left behind for the new owners.

"I haven't eaten lunch, Dorothy. Would you join me?"

"Sure. Are your folks around?"

"No, Daddy wanted to take a drive to Pigeon Forge and cross the mountain into Cherokee. They take that trip every other year," Ellie says. "I would go with them but someone has to be on guard."

I sit down at the breakfast table and clasp my hands.

"Why on guard? Do you have prowlers?" I inquire.

"I don't know if you're aware that a new family has moved into Miss Alicia's cabin. Pete and Marie Brown have troubled teenage boys who are mischievous. I've complained to their mother, but she seems to have no control over them. We have chickens in the barn and enjoy fresh eggs. I'm pretty sure the boys are stealing from us."

"Have you spoken with Detective Galena Chico about the problem?" I inquire as Ellie sets a bowl of soup in front of me.

She shakes her head. "I'd have to file a formal complaint and no way can I walk into that office again without Butch sitting there."

"I understand, death steals the people we love all too often."

"I'm so sorry I blamed you for Lloyd's death," Ellie says as she places her bowl on the table and sits down across the table from me.

"I was crazy with grief," she adds.

"No need to apologize. Lloyd was a great detective."

Ellie swipes her leaky eyes with the back of her hand.

"Let's talk about something else, shall we?"

I taste her soup. "This is delicious."

After eating lunch, we talk about Columbia and how it has grown by leaps and bounds. Tennessee is receiving new residents every day from states like California that charge too many taxes. I'm grateful I decided to stop by to see Ellie. This visit is *Chicken Soup* to my soul.

12

GRAHAM PERKINS IS SEATED on the sofa in his mother's den. He took the afternoon off to discuss how living with her would work.

"You and Cyn can have the upstairs to yourself," Lorene tells him. "You didn't tell me she was pregnant when you married her."

"I know, Mama, we weren't proud of that," he admits. "But traditionally, couples live together today before getting married."

"So, you can try her out to see if she's worthy to be your wife?" Lorene glares at her elderly son, a smart pharmacist that works for Walgreens. "Never mind that I'm old fashioned in my thinking."

Graham stews over her comment before answering.

"My condo has no yard, and Cynthia's apartment is barely large enough for one person," he continues. "You have a great backyard, and while we are living with you, we want to build our own house."

"Here on my farm?" This is news to Lorene.

"Well, yes. Dad did intend for me and Sam to inherit the property—after you passed, of course." He waits for her approval.

"Well, that was kind of Crawford to put that in his will."

"Mama, if you don't want us living with you, just say so. I can get a job in Murfreesboro and we can live with Cynthia's parents."

Lorene's eyes drip with tears. "No, that would be inconvenient if you intend to build a house next door to me. Have you spoken to Sam about your plans?" She wrings a dishtowel like it's a chicken's neck.

"When you pass, you can give Sam this house," Graham says.

The buzzer in the kitchen goes off. "I need to take my cake out of the oven, son. Let me think about all we've talked about. I'll need to redo my will and divide this property equally between you boys."

"Of course, Mama. Take your time. The baby's not due until the middle of June," he says. "Meanwhile, I'll put my condo up for sale."

* * *

It's after two p.m. when I bid Ellie goodbye and drive over to Lorene's house. The front door is unlocked but I knock first before going inside. I find my friend snoozing in Crawford's recliner.

Lorene looks so content. She must be comforted in sitting in the exact spot her deceased husband occupied on a daily basis for so many decades. Hearts on fire need quenching. *Sweet dreams, friend.*

I sit on the sofa quietly waiting for her to wake up. The odor of chocolate lingers in the house. I'm hungry so I tiptoe into the kitchen to find out where the odor is coming from—it's a chocolate cake.

I lift the plastic lid and inhale the chocolate odor.

"What are you doing, Dorothy?"

Startled, I spin around and nearly take a tumble. "Your front door was unlocked," I explain. "I was just admiring your cake."

Lorene yawns. "Let's cut us a piece, I'm hungry."

"Are you sure? Is the cake for something or someone special?"

"It's for me," she says in a surly tone of voice. "I like desserts."

"Okay." I won't argue with a disgruntled old woman.

Lorene removes a long, serrated knife from the kitchen drawer and begins slicing the cake. "Just a small piece for me, please."

"Nobody's watching your figure, Dorothy."

I draw in my neck, offended. "I'm careful how I look."

"Why?" She lays an ample-sized piece of cake on a ceramic plate and passes it across the kitchen bar. "Tom isn't coming back."

I cringe at her words. "He might fool us all; he's undercover."

"Did you sleep with him? Is this what your attachment is all about? Do you think he's going to marry a woman old enough to be his mother?" Lorene is mean and I want to slap my best friend hard.

To lighten her remark, I chuckle. "I'll tell you what I told Claire when she asked if I'd slept with Thomas Kessler."

Lorene licks chocolate icing off her fingers. "What?"

"What happens undercover stays there," I reply.

"Cute."

We eat our cake in silence.

"You have coffee made?" I inquire.

"I'll make some fresh decaf." She hops up to accomplish the task.

We take our coffees into the den and sit down.

"Now," I say, "what is really troubling you, my friend?"

"Graham and Cynthia are moving in with me."

"Okay." I realize this is likely the secret Alicia kept from me.

"It's not a bad thing, actually." Lorene rolls her eyes. "I can use the help around the house—until the baby comes, and then—"

"Come again?" I interrupt, scrubbing one ear with a finger.

"I'm going to be a grandmother in June."

"That's wonderful, Lorene! You will love that."

"Graham wants to build a house on my property."

"So, you'll have family close to help out with the farm chores."

"No, I'll have to hire a housekeeper. Cyn and Graham have jobs. I can't see our county coroner staying home to take care of a baby."

"Are you thinking of the added expense it will incur?"

"Utilities, food—that and my lack of privacy. Where will you stay when you come for a visit? I'm giving Graham the run of upstairs."

I throw a hand. "Don't worry about me; I can sleep on the sofa or share a bed with you. Crawford won't mind," I add.

"I suppose . . ."

I can see Lorene is burdened with decisions.

"Look, take a day at a time. You can work out the details with your lawyer—how your property will be divided between your sons."

"I know—it's just overwhelming. I'm used to quiet."

"I plan to buy my own place soon, so you can come and spend time with me if your home feels too crowded," I offer.

"In Nashville, or here?" Lorene asks.

"You know my daughter is bent on me living close to her as I get older. I visited Alicia this morning. Her apartment is nice, too."

"I thought you sold your house so you could travel."

"Well, the best-made plans don't always pan out."

After getting a Christmas card from Moscow, Russia, I expected Tom to show up and rescue me. But no word since. Then, he operates undercover, so maybe it's impossible for him to contact me again.

"I guess we both have a lot to think about," Lorene says. "I'm sorry I've been so harsh with you. We've always weathered trials together." She looks longingly at me. "We will again, my friend."

"Yes, we will."

With that problem discussed and behind us, I tell Lorene about Ellie's problem with the two teenage boys that live in Alicia's cabin behind her house. "She's nervous about being alone," I explain.

"Well, I would be, too. She should talk to the police about the problem," Lorene pipes. "Those boys might break into her house one night and steal something besides chicken eggs."

"I already suggested that. Ellie wants me to stay with her."

"Tonight, or all the time?" Lorene reacts.

"Tonight. Maybe two nights, until her parents get home from their vacation to the Smokies. What else do I have to do?"

"I was looking forward to ordering a pizza so we could watch an old Elvis movie," Lorene says. "I don't want to be alone tonight."

I sigh and evaluate my choices. I'm Lorene's best friend and she's worried about her safety. Yet, Ellie is scared, too. Who do I help?

"I think I have the solution. Why don't you spend the night at Ellies with me?" I suggest. "I'm sure she won't mind. We can have a girl's slumber party—just like we did when we were in high school."

"Okay, but phone and ask her first," Lorene insists.

I remove my cellphone from my purse and make the call. Lorene stares at me as Ellie and I parlay. I end the call and smile.

"She says it's a great idea, for us to come over anytime." I glance at the time. "It's after 3:30 p.m. What do you think?"

"I'll pack a bag. Where is yours?" Lorene inquires.

"In the trunk of my car. I always go prepared."

13

IT IS DARK BY SEVEN thirty and thunder rumbles in the distance.

"I didn't know it was going to storm tonight," Lorene remarks as Ellie and I sit with her in the den. "I hope it isn't a terrible storm."

I know she's thinking of the time when several tornadoes marched through Maury County and destroyed multiple properties. Including this house. "Just an ordinary thunder-boomer," I tell her. "April showers bring May flowers." Our gazes lock and I see fear in her gaze.

"We'll be fine, Lorene," Ellie assures her.

"Besides, tornadoes don't strike twice," I predict, feeling more at home sitting here in Ellie's recliner than anywhere else. Perhaps I made a mistake in selling the property Arthur and I shared for decades.

"I recall those awful tornadoes that passed through Columbia last year," Ellie comments. "You were dating Clint Howard."

"We weren't dating, Ellie. We are just good friends."

"He was here with you at the house when your roof caved in," Lorene recalls. "You said "are" but I thought he was dead."

"No proof he is." If not, who sent me the Christmas card from Russia? I refuse to give up hope that I will see Clint/Tom again.

"Butch never told me why Clint came to Columbia," Ellie says.

"Life is full of mysteries." I give Ellie no further explanation.

Lorene knows that Clint is a.k.a. Thomas Kessler, an undercover CIA agent sent to Columbia to watch my back when a Mafia assassin escaped from prison. I later learned that Tom volunteered for the job because I resembled his deceased wife Angela, murdered by the same assassin who ended the lives of my Arthur and Crawford Perkins.

Lightning strikes close by and the bones of the house shutter.

"That was close!" Lorene exclaims as rain thunders down on the new roof. "Did you roll up all your car windows, Dorothy?"

Double D-D! "No, I didn't." I clamor to my feet and rush to the foyer, out the door into the pouring rain, and scramble to my car.

The front seat is as soaked as I am. I start the engine and close the two front windows I left cracked for ventilation. Ellie and Lorene stand in the doorway laughing at me as I hustle to take cover under the porch. Louisiana deluges can't compete with this downpour.

I lean over and shake out my hair, longer than usual.

"You smell like a wet dog," Lorene hails, snickering.

"I'll need to shower and change clothes before supper."

I hurry up the stairs to the hall bath and shimmy out of my wet duds. As I blast the shower with hot water, I note that Ellie has fresh soap and towels sitting on the counter. I hop in the shower.

Thirty minutes later I am dry-dressed and downstairs. I find Ellie and Lorene in the kitchen. Ellie is slicing a deluxe pizza.

"Something smells delicious." I announce my presence.

"Domino's Pizza," Ellie replies, tossing me a look. "I ordered it soon after I found out you girls were spending the night with me."

It is still raining outside, though the storm has passed over.

"Where is my little dog?" I inquire.

"Pepper?" Ellie sets the pizza cutter down beside our food. "Mama took him with them to the mountains. She's fallen in love with that little terrier. He sleeps on the end of their bed at nights."

I was never a dog person, so I'm relieved Pepper has a good home. Lorene meant well when she gifted me the terrier after Arthur passed.

"How does your father feel about that?"

"Dad?" Ellie huffs. "Whatever Mama says is good for him."

"Arthur was like that, too. Easy going." I think of how hard it is to understand Tom, a huge mystery to me. "I miss him terribly."

Both of them, actually.

Ellie sniffles. "I wasn't legally married to Butch, but we were a couple for two years. I'll never find another man to replace him."

"You might." God knows at my age if I can fall in love so can Ellie. "Love has no age qualifications." I look at Lorene.

"No, no, no! Not me," she protests. "I am happy flying solo."

We eat our pizza and settle down in the den to watch "Love Me Tender," the Elvis Presley movie that depicts a Confederate team ordered to rob a Union payroll train. Except the Civil War ends, and the team is left with the loot. The Feds come after them.

It's a long movie in comparison to modern flicks. Ellie fell asleep half way through, but Lorene and I could not take our eyes off of Elvis, that handsome young actor that made it huge in early rock music.

I cut off the television and cover Ellie with an Afghan.

Lorene yawns. "What time is it?" She squints at the wall clock.

"Not really late, 9:50," I note.

"I've been up since five this morning so I'm going to bed."

Lorene walks through the kitchen and disappears through the doorway that leads to the long hall to the front of the house. The stairs leading to the second level begin in the foyer. I'm not sleepy.

I walk into the kitchen and open the backdoor to the porch. The rain has finally stopped and a cool breeze blows debris across the yard. I want to see the chickens in the barn, so I quietly slip outdoors.

A sliver of a moon reminds me of a rocking chair. Clouds meander across the sky highlighted white by the peek-a-boo moon. I want to reverse time and go back twenty years in order to make better choices. My son Lance would still be alive. Maybe I could convince him to see a doctor and have his cholesterol checked. I would tell him to eat more healthily. Maybe he would not have had a heart attack at age fifty-one.

The day Arthur was murdered by Crystal Creek? I would forbid him to leave the house the entire day. If I could change one thing in the past, maybe everything else would be altered going forward.

I am standing at the door of the barn before I realize it.

I listen through the door and hear clucking. A hen cackles and I suspect one of the mischievous boys that lives in Alicia's former cabin is inside stealing eggs again. I open the door and surprise slaps me.

There's a huge black man standing there.

"Who are you?" I refuse to be intimidated.

I can only see his white teeth shining in the dark barn.

"Dorothy Powell. So, we finally meet."

"Who are you?"

"I am called by many names."

"Thief is one, I suspect. Ellie would give you some eggs if you asked her." I don't want to become this huge man's enemy.

"I'm surprised to see you here," he says, stepping closer.

He's muscular built, in his thirties, my guess.

"Touché," I respond.

"Dorothy, are you out here?"

"That is Ellie. Do you want to ask her if it's okay to borrow some eggs?" I am super cool under this uncomfortable situation.

The barn door opens and I turn around.

"What are you doing out here?" Ellie asks me.

"Ask him what he's doing." I turn around and the man is gone.

"What do you mean? Did you see someone out here?"

I think about my answer. I don't want to frighten Ellie even more than she already is. I will talk to Detective Chico tomorrow about the man in the barn. Ellie asks, "What did you see, Dorothy?"

"It must have been my imagination." I turn her around with a hand. "We should go back inside the house, dear. All is fine out here."

It isn't fine, and I don't know what to make of the black man.

14

Thursday, May 11

I DID NOT GET A WINK of sound sleep last night. I was in and out of foggy dreams that made no sense whatsoever. The black man in Ellie's barn was real, but I have yet to determine if he poses a danger.

I am seated at Ellie's breakfast table shortly after eight a.m. A plate of pancakes slathered in Maple syrup sits untouched in front of me. My thoughts are too heavy for my stomach to digest food.

Lorene ignores her food while sipping on coffee.

"Aren't you girls hungry?" Ellie asks. "We didn't have a big supper last night." She forks a slice of pancake into her mouth. "I'm not a gourmet cook, but I know for a fact that Aunt Jemima is."

"Cute," Lorene pipes, referring to the pancake label.

"How did you sleep, Lorene?" I see her tired eyes.

"Not the best." She piddles with her fork, stirring syrup around in her plate. "I need more coffee. Can I get either of you a fresh cup?"

"No thank you." My untouched cup of Joe is cold.

"Is it the storm that bothered you?" Ellie asks Lorene.

"No, it's the storm moving into her life," I answer for her.

"Oh." Ellie looks at me. "Is it something you can share?"

"Lorene?" I need her permission.

She shakes her head no at me.

"Better we talk about it another time," I tell Ellie.

"Okay, now that we've settled that," Ellie says, "what's bothering you, Dorothy? Did something in the barn spook you last night?"

"Did I miss something exciting?" Lorene perks up as she returns from the kitchen with a refill in her coffee cup.

"Why did you go out there?" Ellie inquires. "Noises?"

"No noises, just wanted to see the chickens," I reply.

Lorene shoves her plate aside and blows on the surface of her piping-hot cup of coffee before taking a sip. "You miss Arthur."

"Yes, I do. Last night the weather was nice and cool after the rain, and I just felt like going outdoors and looking up at the moon."

"Okay." Ellie is satisfied with my explanation of a night excursion. "You're sure you didn't see one of those naughty boys?"

"No naughty boys," I say, getting up from the table.

"Where are you going?" Lorene asks.

"Aren't we going back to your house? I have things I need to do today." I intend to visit Detective Chico and tell her about the black man in Ellie's barn. Plus, I want to know if she's learned anything new about the employee at Coffee Call who tried to kill me.

To my question, Lorene replies, "I'll be upstairs shortly to pack."

"I wish you girls wouldn't rush off so soon," Ellie says.

I know she is lonely for Lloyd. "We'll stay over another time."

"Please do." Ellie picks up our plates and takes them to the sink.

I go up the stairs and brush my teeth in the bathroom. My Bible is tucked inside my overnight bag so I remove it to read a passage from Psalms. I love King David's viewpoint of life. No matter who hated him, or tried to kill him, he always trusted God to order his steps.

Lorene finds me in the bedroom fifteen minutes later. "Are you ready to go back to my house?" she inquires, her overnight bag in hand.

"Yes." I close my Bible. "I'm armed with the Sword of the Spirit and ready to face this cruel world," I declare and follow her downstairs.

Ellie hugs us both goodbye and invites us to come for another visit soon. We are parked in front of Lorene's house ten minutes later.

"What is Sam doing here?" Lorene exits the passenger side of my car. Her front door stands open as she approaches the house.

Sam staggers out the door, coughing. Alarm drives me to quick action as I dash from the car toward him to offer assistance.

"What happened, Sam?" I ask while Lorene is frozen in time.

He mutters something as Lorene resumes motion again, steps on the porch, and grabs her youngest son's arm. "What did you just say?"

Sam coughs and spits at the side of the porch. "Gas leak."

"What?" I step into the foyer and get a whiff of suffocating gas.

In reaction, my eyes burn and the odor sets me off coughing hard and gasping for breath as I hurry back out on the porch for fresh air.

"I just had the gas guy check my tank," Lorene utters.

"When was that, Mama?" Sam struggles to breathe.

"He came early yesterday morning," she replies.

"Did the Columbia Gas Authority phone to say he was coming?"

"No, the guy said there had been some leaks in the main line and was routinely checking properties along the highway," Lorene explains.

"Where was the leak, Sam?" I ask.

"The gas eye was turned on—not lit," he replies.

"I didn't do it, son, I swear," Lorene declares.

"Who else has a key to your house?" I query Lorene.

"Besides us, only my two sons," Lorene replies.

"Sam, have you called the police?" I ask.

"No." He exhibits alarm. "You think someone broke in the house and purposely turned on the gas stove?"

I nod my head. A few seconds of silence ensues.

"If you had not been here first, Sam, and Lorene had gone inside the house and flipped on a light, what would have happened?"

"There would have been an explosion."

I lock eyes with Lorene. "Somebody tried to kill me," she says.

"No, Lorene. Somebody tried to kill me. They knew I was with you. They must have followed us to Ellie's house yesterday then came back here to do their dirty work." I am so angry I could spit nails.

Lorene is crying and Sam is holding her.

"It must have been that black man," I sputter.

"What black man?" Lorene and Sam simultaneously utter.

"He was in Ellie's barn last night," I reveal. "We should go and talk to Detective Chico about what just happened. Sam?"

"I have to go to work, Mama."

"It's okay, son, we can do this alone." She stares a moment. "What prompted you to come to my house this morning?"

"Just a feeling . . ." he says, shaking his head.

"That was the Holy Spirit, Sam. He was protecting me and Lorene. God is so good. He's always on the side of a Christian." I give the lad a hug. "Thank you for caring so much."

He nods, scrubs a tear off one cheek.

15

LORENE OPENS ALL THE windows in the den and kitchen to air out the gas odor while I sit on the back porch trying to understand why it is so important that I die before my time. Is this about Thomas Kessler? Because he cares about my welfare. This second attempt on my life confirms that he lives. We both are hated by the Russian Mafia.

"Do you want to eat something before we go into town?"

"Thinking we could have been killed in an explosion doesn't do much for my appetite," I admit. "But thanks anyway."

I abandon the swing and go back in the house.

"Do you think we should call Detective Chico before we barge into her office?" Lorene asks as she closes the open windows.

"I think our first call should be to a locksmith," I say. "I want you to change all your outdoor locks and enter a new password in your security system—which I remind you did not go off." I glare at her.

She shrinks in shame. "I forgot to set it last night before we left for Ellie's." My hug seems to say to her, "It's all right."

"Better, I'll ask Graham to take care of that task, Dorothy," Lorene decides, her morale suddenly bolstered by our new mission.

"You're right, we need to talk to Detective Chico pronto."

* * *

CIA Director Jackson Carlton, Jack to his agents, is seated at his desk in the Pentagon conversing with Charlie Darby, Thomas Kessler's closest confidante. "And you've heard nothing from Tom?"

"Zip," Charlie replies.

"When did he last text you?" Jack inquires.

"Early February."

"The last report I received was at the end of December," Jack says. "Do you think Tom was made by the Russians and arrested?"

Charlie shrugs. *I don't know.*

"Who do we have to send over there and check?"

"Why not Drop-Dead-Gorgeous?" Charlie suggests.

"Kelly Knotts." Jack nods. "She's new, but was at the top of her class. As you know, she came over from the FBI."

"She's beautiful, charming, and can wiggle her way into the Russian Mafia before they realize what has hit them," Charlie says.

"Okay then, I'll ask her if she wants the assignment," Jack decides.

* * *

Dorothy and Lorene are at the city precinct, downstairs trying to convince Jake the Guard that they need to go up to the second floor. No, they do not have an appointment, why doesn't he call up to Detective Galena Chico's office and ask her if she'll see them?

Finally, he makes the call. Nods, then hangs up.

"Go on up, ladies."

"Thank you, Jake, that is so kind of you," Lorene sweetly says.

I want to clobber him for taking so much of our time. But I see the moony look in my friend's eyes. She's warming up to a romantic relationship. And it's about time; it's no fun living in a house alone.

On our way up on the elevator, I say, "Lorene? Jake is too young for you. He's got to be in his early sixties."

"You are one to talk!" She shoots back. "Cradle robber!"

The double doors shutter open and save our butts from ruining a perfectly wonderful friendship. We both decide to drop the matter.

Detective Chico is standing in the hall in front of the open door to her office. "What is so urgent, ladies?"

"Can we come in and discuss our grievance in person?" I ask.

She waves her hand like it's a magic wand and we float past her good-looking male secretary and enter her private office. She shuts the door and takes a seat at her desk leaving us standing.

No chairs are available for sitting.

"I have five minutes," Detective Chico defines our visit.

"Someone tried to kill us this morning," Lorene spurts.

"Really?" Chico smirks, assuming we are old fools.

"Really!" I forcefully say. "We would not be here otherwise."

Chico phones Blake and tells him to order lattes from Coffee Call and to hold all her calls. "Now, exactly what happened, ladies?"

I take charge and explain what took place from the time we left Lorene's house late Tuesday to spend the night with Ellie Simpson until the time we returned this morning around eight a.m.

Lorene can no longer sit quietly. "If my son Sam had not had a premonition that I needed help, Dorothy and I would be up in smoke."

I think she's the one who should be writing a novel—she has such a way with words. I add, "Someone broke into the house during the night and turned on the gas range. Unlit. Sam identified the problem."

Chico nods. "Dorothy—"

"I know, my great-granddaughter June wonders why I'm always getting into so much trouble. All I can come up with is the Russian Mafia likes to get even when someone troubles their operations."

Chico twists her plump pink lips while assessing my opinion.

"If you know something, Detective Chico, you should tell us."

I am proud of Lorene, so brave to demand cooperation.

"We—meaning our team—found a connection between our dead Coffee Call server and the Kentucky branch of the Russian Mafia."

"Really?" I feel confirmation of my suspicions.

"Danny Mason is the big boss's grand-nephew."

"The big boss that the TBI shot and killed?" I want clarification.

Chico nods, her dark eyes skittering between me and Lorene.

"Then why did someone kill Danny?" Lorene asks.

"You fail with the Mafia, you don't survive," Chico replies.

"I still don't get why killing me is so important. I don't know anything," I report. "I don't want to know anything. And if I did, I certainly would not poke my nose into the slightest part of their dirty business. I should write them a letter and clarify my position."

Detective Chico chuckles. "Anything else to add to this drama?"

"Yes," I reply, and tell her about the black man in Ellie's barn.

Chico clamps her mouth with one hand as a knock is at the door. "Come in, Blake." And he does, with the three lattes she ordered.

A latte to die for, I think, then wonder if the Mafia has sent in a new guy or gal to Coffee Call that knows how to mix a lethal drink.

Blake passes out the coffees. I hold mine in my hand, unsure if I'm brave enough to take the first sip. I do not know Blake that well.

"Oh, give me the blame thing!" Lorene switches Styrofoam cups with me. Lest I protest, I accept her gracious gift and sip the foam off the top. We chitchat a few more minutes than leave Chico to her devices. I am actually hungry now that I've gotten a load off my chest.

We are in my car when I suggest we have seafood for lunch. Lorene agrees, hungry, too. A brush with death has strange effects of people. One never knows when their last meal will be set before them.

"Maybe we should pick up Alicia and take her with us to lunch."

"Good idea." I check the time.

"I doubt she eats lunch this early," Lorene says. "It's only 10:30."

"We'll take our time."

So, as friends do, we carry out our luncheon plans successfully.

And hopefully, this time, no one dies.

16

Friday, May 12

I HAD SPENT THE remainder of yesterday afternoon at Lorene's house while a locksmith changed out all the door locks and a new passcode had been entered into her security system. Sam planned on spending Thursday night, so I had left for Claire's house around seven.

I'm a bit tattered after our near accident yesterday, so I'd slept in. I crept into the den and discovered Claire lying on the sofa.

It didn't take long to recognize my daughter was distraught and had been crying for a while. Her blue eyes were bloodshot and crow's feet radiated from the corners. "What's wrong, Claire?"

"Ted did not come home last night." She sniffles.

"Did you two have a fight?"

"No, but we hardly spoke at breakfast yesterday."

"Why not?" Marriages are made or broken on conversations.

"I was miffed." She sniffles again. "Two days ago, he came home again with lipstick on his shirt collar. And the perfume wasn't mine."

"Oh." What else could I add to that?

If he is cheating, he's not good at it, I form an opinion.

"Ted's going to leave me, Mama."

I try to take in all the drama at once and it makes me dizzy. I sure can't tell her there was an attempt on my life again.

She sobers and glares at me. "Why aren't you saying something?"

I shrug my shoulders.

"Aren't you going to tell me we need to see a marriage counselor?"

A Kleenex box is nearby and Claire snags one.

"Have you phoned Ted? Maybe he got sick. Have you checked the hospitals? Maybe he had an accident and can't call you."

Her gaze widens. "No, I didn't think of that."

"Call his secretary and ask when she last spoke to him," I suggest.

She nods. The number of his office landline is programmed into her iPhone. "Darlene, Ted didn't come home last night, do you know where he is?" she inquires, her eyes locked on me for support.

I motion for her to turn on the speaker system.

"Mr. Burke had an appointment in Crossville at three p.m. yesterday," Darlene tells Claire. "He did not return to the office."

"Okay, thank you."

"Wait! Is Mr. Burke all right?" Darlene asks.

"I don't know. But I intend to find out," Claire replies.

The call ends. "He's with the other woman," she pipes.

"You don't know that. Call his cell phone again."

"I've already tried multiple times; he doesn't want to talk to me," Claire reports. But she makes the call anyhow.

"Hello."

"It's Ted," Claire whispers to me.

"Honey, are you okay? Where are you?"

Claire turns up the speaker system so I can hear better.

"At a motel somewhere thirty miles east of Nashville," he replies. "I had an accident, Claire. The car was totaled. The EMT guys came and checked me out, gave me meds for sore ribs, and brought me to this rundown motel that must have been built fifty years ago."

"Oh, honey, I am so sorry," Claire says. "I stayed up most of the night worrying about you." I note she does not say she thinks he was screwing another woman. My Claire is smarter than that.

"My phone was smashed. I just got a new one delivered."

I splay my hands. *See . . . it's never quite as bad as you think.*

"I'll get in the car and come and get you. What's the address?" Claire asks, then writes down the information to enter into her phone.

I sigh. At least, the worst scenario has not occurred at the Burke's residence. Physical wounds will heal; emotional ones maybe never.

I suspect these two love each other but are experiencing a self-awareness after their children have left the nest. Parents need to fulfill some individual lifetime goals while living peaceably and respecting each other's views as they emerge into a new chapter in their lives.

All of this philosophic thought gives me a headache.

"Want to take a ride with me?" Claire asks before retreating to her bedroom to get dressed. "We can stop for breakfast somewhere."

"No thank you, dear." I'm thinking of calling a realtor to see property today. I promised Claire I would, and I need my own space. So do Ted and Claire. So does Lorene since Graham and Cynthia are moving in with her. Life is changing again. I pray all will be good.

But what about the killer still out there, stalking me?

The house is quiet after Claire leaves to pick up Ted. I am about to phone a realtor to look at condos in Brentwood, hoping to get a unit in a senior-citizen-only complex. I don't want to listen to children screaming outside my window. I don't want to live on a golf course where loose balls fly askew and attack my property. But I don't get the chance to contact a realtor because Claire's landline rings and I am prompted to answer it. It could be important. "Hello."

"Mrs. Burke?"

"No, this is Dorothy Powell, Claire's mother."

"Mrs. Powell, where is your daughter? She was supposed to pick up Billy from his elementary school at nine. I've called her cell phone but she isn't answering. All the other children have gone home."

"What do you want me to do?" I ask, perturbed at Claire for not checking her daily calendar before she left the house.

"Will you come and get him?" the woman asks.

"Are you Billy's teacher?"

"No, I'm Laura Prescott, the principle of Brentwood Elementary," she replies. "Like I said, our school is closed."

"Why?"

"There's a state teachers conference in Knoxville today."

"Then why did you allow children to come to school in the first place if you knew they would be dismissed by nine o'clock?" I will never understand why so-called smart people act as they do.

"We've used up all our snow days," she explains.

I am exasperated. After someone has tried to nuke me in a gas explosion, I feel unequipped to entertain an eight-year-old boy, even if he is my great grandson. June was a handful on Monday.

"Have you contacted his mother?" I will use every instrument in my mental toolbox to avoid looking after Billy today.

"She's in a meeting and can't be disturbed."

I search for a reason why I am unavailable for this task. Short of lying, I have no excuse. "Okay, I will come and get him."

Scouting for a property will have to wait another day. The drive over to the elementary school takes less than fifteen minutes. Principal Prescott doesn't have a pleasant expression on her less-than-lovely face. I will be kind and try not to judge her current state of beauty.

Billy's cheeks are red. He's been crying. If he calls me GG like his little sister did, I am going to scream. I park my BMW on the curb, leave the motor humming and walk over to my great grandson.

"We'll see you tomorrow, Billy. Have a nice day," the principal says. Then gives me a look that scalds before she walks away.

"Where's my Granny?" Billy asks.

"She went to fetch your grandfather." I grasp his small hand and lead him to my car. Unfortunately, I don't have a car seat.

I open the back door and Billy stands there.

"What is it, Billy? You need help climbing in?" I query.

"I can't ride in your car; you don't have a car seat. It's not safe. Mommy says to never ride in a car unless you are buckled up."

"Well, Mommy isn't here, and your grandmother is busy, so get in the backseat," I tell him. "We'll stop for ice cream on our way home."

"Okay, GG." He grits his teeth but obeys.

17

I FINALLY CONTACT HELEN at noon when she takes a break from her meeting. "Billy's here with me. Can you come get him?"

"I can't," my granddaughter replies. "Where's Mama?"

"Your daddy had an automobile accident yesterday, so she's gone to fetch him," I explain. "He's bummed up but not seriously injured."

"How did that happen?"

"I don't know all the details, talk to your mother."

"Okay, can you keep Billy until I get off work at five?"

"Is it all right if he looks at property with me?" I ask.

"Do you have a car seat? It's against the law to drive a child around Nashville without one." Helen falls silent, distrusting me. But I am relieved she does not call me MMM. *My Mother's Mother.*

"I will purchase one from Walmart, Helen, so not to worry."

Billy tugs on the hem of my shirt.

"Not now, Billy." I swipe his hand away.

"Check the garage," Helen suggests. "Mama was talking about buying a larger car seat last weekend since June is growing so fast."

Billy tugs on the hem of my shirt again, hooking me with a finger to lean a closer. "Ask Mommy if we can have Mickey Dee's for lunch."

He sticks his thumb in his mouth and doesn't pull out a plum. I am ready to pull out my hair if my teeth don't fall out first.

"I heard that," Helen says. "Sure, get him a burger—anything to make life easier for you, GG. I will pick up Billy around five thirty."

She called me GG. June rules that household.

"Oh, if Mama and Daddy come home, you can carry on with your plans for the day," Helen kindly offers, like she's my personal secretary.

The call ends and I think about what my granddaughter said. *Carry on with your plans for the day?* There will be only an hour of sunlight left to carry on with my plans for the day by five thirty. *Horse radish!*

* * *

After hearing what happened at Lorene Perkins' house, Detective Chico sets up an appointment with Captain Colbert on Friday. Two recent murders, plus two attempts to end Dorothy Powell's life, complicates how to proceed with investigating the death of Gloria Ann Bolton. Her husband Gerry has called every day for an update on the case but Galena has nothing to report. Maybe it had been unwise to have told Mrs. Powell that the deceased Danny Mason was the nephew of Leonard Stoldt, the former Russian Mafia boss for Kentucky.

Didn't Mrs. Powell deserve to know the truth?

However, until a crime has been committed, legally surveilling her or placing her in protective custody was not an option. The only way she can protect herself is to proceed cautiously day by day.

Captain Marilyn Colbert has fifteen minutes to spare at 2:30 that afternoon, so Galena waits for her to return. Mayor Carson Pierce's wife had a confrontation with a staff member who went ballistic and threatened her life. The mayor wanted to know how to proceed with filing a complaint against the man. At least, that was the office buzz.

Marilyn flew into the office like a bat out of hell. "Oh, Detective Chico, I forgot you were coming." She shews Galena into her private office and slams the door. "Politics! I hate the word."

"If this is not a good time—"

"No time is good," Marilyn quips, "what have you got for me?"

Galena sits down and relays to the captain what she'd been told by Lorene Perkins and Dorothy Powell yesterday. Marilyn listens attentively while tapping her ballpoint pen on her calendar pad.

"Do we have the legal responsibility to protect Mrs. Powell?"

"Has a crime been committed?" Marilyn inquires.

"Indirectly, yes. Someone tried to blow up Mrs. Perkins' house," Galena replied. "But . . . maybe Dorothy just happened to be there."

"Yes, there is that," Marilyn says, always a quick study.

"I could have someone follow Mrs. Powell for forty-eight hours and see what happens—watch her back for anything unusual."

"What about the black man Mrs. Powell saw in Ellie Simpson's barn? Do you think it was Dom with a funny last name?" Marilyn asks.

"He made no move to hurt her," Galena points out.

"You said Ellie showed up in the barn, so maybe that's what saved Mrs. Powell this time," Marilyn points out. "Put someone on her."

"Thank you. I feel somewhat responsible for her safety." Galena is relieved. "I have someone in mind who has ghostly talent."

Captain Colbert chuckles. "We're sure to eventually lose him to the TBI or the blame CIA. Are you speaking of Joseph Hale?"

"Yes, he's requested grunt work for training," Galena reveals.

"Are you absolutely sure?"

"I am," Galena replies. "Doesn't matter that he's the son of the infamous prosecutor that defends criminals in Nashville courts, Joseph is young and hungry for making his own fame."

"Okay. Tell him to keep his distance from Mrs. Powell. She's old but smart, and I don't want him getting hurt. Does she own a gun?"

"I have no idea. The Second Amendment is in full force in Tennessee. Most don't even have a permit to carry," Galena pipes.

"Okay, Detective Chico, carry on . . ."

* * *

Claire is back at the house with Ted by 3:30, mid-afternoon. Little Billy ate all of his Mickey Dee's burger plus an order of salty fries and fell asleep in the backseat of my BMW in Claire's new car seat.

"Helen texted me you were watching Billy. Where is he?"

"Sleeping in the back of my car in your garage," I answer.

"He will get too hot and get sick, Mama," Claire fusses.

"Hi, Ted," I say as he slumps over at the breakfast bar, chugging down a cold Coke like he's desert dry. "Sorry about your wreck."

"It's okay, Mama, I'm still kicking." He half smiles.

Barely kicking, I think to myself.

"I'd better go get Billy. How long has he been sleeping?" Claire asks, the concerned grandmother who doesn't trust her own mother.

"Two hours—poor kid is sleep deprived," I say.

"I'm going to bed, Claire." Ted limps through the den and disappears through Door One. I know there is a short hallway, so he will pass through Door Two into his master bedroom, then walk through Door Three, his bathroom, to pee. Then he'll crash in bed.

I wonder why my quirky mind processed that event. Does that mean I am old? Do I have dementia? Why does where Ted walks, or what he does matter? It's wasted thought. It's foolish banter.

"Mama?"

I realize Claire is speaking to me. "What, dear?"

"Are you having a senior moment?"

"Nope, just a crazy one. Not to worry, dear."

18

TOO LATE IN THE DAY to call a realtor and see property, I decide to drive back to Columbia and visit Ellie Simpson again.

She opens the backdoor, surprised to see me so soon.

"Did someone die?" she asks.

I chuckle. "A little of me, piece by piece." I make light of her comment. I know my time dwindles, but what I do with it matters.

"Come in and say hello to Dad and Mom. They just returned from their trip to the Smokies." Ellie's door invitingly stands open.

Wes and Jasmine Parks had sold their home in Chicago, Illinois, and moved in with Ellie the day after I signed over my property. I still feel like this house owns a part of me. I'm sure Arthur walks the cow pasture sometimes if he gets bored with music in Heaven. Never one to sing or hum a tune, no telling how he fits in that crowd.

Ellie holds out her coffee cup. "Just made, do you want some?"

"No thanks." I tramp into the den with a smile on my face and sadness tucked away in my heart. I won't let them see my profound distress. "I hope you enjoyed your trip to the mountains!" I gush.

"Oh, it was magnificent!" Jasmine abandons the sofa to give me a tight hug. "Ellie told me you and your friend Lorene spent the night."

"Yes," I glance at Wes and nod to acknowledge his presence. "That is why I am here. I need to alert you folks to a situation."

Boy, that statement wiped the smiles off their faces. I felt like Santa Claus in reverse—no gifts and about to deliver bad news.

Ellie sits on the cuff of the sofa, a hand on her mother's back.

Wes's gray eyes survey me then he asks, "What kind of situation?"

I limp over to a straight-back chair and plant my butt in it firmly, cross my legs, then contemplate how to answer that pertinent question.

"The other night, when I was in the barn . . ."

"I remember," Ellie says, her bright emerald eyes wide and alert.

"Well, what I didn't tell you was I saw a big black man standing in the shadows. When you suddenly came into the barn he backed off."

"Backed off?" Jasmine softly repeated my words.

"Yes, he knew my name. I don't know if he would have attacked me had Ellie not shown up," I explain. "But then, he simply left."

"Have you reported the incident to the police?" Wes inquires.

"Yes, after Lorene and I were nearly blown to bits and pieces."

"What?" Ellie stands up and drops her coffee cup.

"When Lorene and I arrived at her house the next morning after we spent the night with you, her son Sam was stumbling out the front door. He'd discovered a gas leak—the oven-range eye was turned on without the pilot light lit. Had he not been there and Lorene flipped on a light . . ." I fold my lips into my mouth. "I wouldn't be here."

Jasmine clamps her lips with a tight hand. "Lorene left the stove on? What was she thinking? Before leaving, she should've checked."

"It wasn't Lorene," I tell Jasmine. "We believe someone broke into our house and purposely intended to hurt us. Me, in particular."

"Are you saying it was an attempted murder?" Wes queries.

"Yes. It's not the first time someone tried to kill me." I explain to Ellie's parents how Gloria Bolton ended up dead instead of me.

Jasmine looks up at her daughter. "And you didn't know this?"

"No, Mama. I would have told you and Dad if I had."

"Are we in danger, too?" Wes asks.

"I can't say for certain, but I don't think so. The black man probably followed Lorene and me over here late Wednesday then returned to her house to set the stage for a deadly gas explosion."

"What are the police doing about all of this?" Ellie quips.

"Lorene and I spoke to Detective Chico and told her everything. Until there is an actual crime, no one is watching my back."

"They may be, Dorothy, but didn't tell you," Wes suggests.

I sigh. "I hope so. Lorene, too. I worry her association with me will get her killed." It's a sad commentary for a long-term friendship.

"Anything we can do to help you, Dorothy?" Wes kindly asks.

"No. I just thought you should know. I should go now."

"Go where? Stay for supper, at least," Ellie says.

"Thanks, but I need to be alone to think. Next time?"

"Sure." Ellie gets up and hugs me. "Walk carefully."

"I will." And carry a big stick, I think to myself. I should purchase a weapon and take lessons. If Tom were here, he'd teach me.

I drive away from the house then turn onto a dirt road that leads me to the pasture where Arthur's cows grazed. The sun is sinking on the horizon leaving streaks of color like waving flags. I love this time of day when daylight dwindles and emerges into the shadows of darkness. Where forest trees become skeletons against a murky mist.

My BMW stands like a lone wolf in the grassy field. I stare up at the sky and wait for the planet Venus to appear. The wind kicks up as sunlight washes away in color, making way for approaching darkness.

"Hi, Arthur." I look up, hoping he can hear me. "I just wanted to say that I miss you. Just because I love Tom Kessler, too, doesn't mean I still don't love you with all my heart. I miss you terribly."

I sit down in the grassy pasture and wonder if I can get back up. I'm not a young chick anymore. My bones creak and arthritis eats at my cartilage. Even a facelift won't rid me completely of wrinkles.

It is pitch dark, no moon to light the way, when I press my hands against the grassy floor and push up. I feel better—don't know why. I think God must be smiling down at me. I've spent the past hour praying for guidance. The stars are out in full like an army of lights.

"Good!" I say as I stand up and stagger back to my car.

Now, I will go over and talk to my friend about a divorce.

19

"YOU WANT WHAT?" LORENE scrubs her right ear like it is lodged with wax. "Are you crazy, Dorothy?"

"Yeah, but don't lock me up yet." I chuckle. "You need to divorce yourself from me. I'm too dangerous to be around. Death chases me and I don't want you caught in its web. It's for the best, for now."

"No," Lorene says. "No way. I won't lose my best friend because some creep is stalking you. We'll fight this beast together, you hear?"

"I need to leave." I have been standing at the door while I tell Lorene my decision. "When the black man is caught, I'll be back."

Lorene wrings her hands, tears streaming down her face.

"Don't do this to me, Dorothy. Please!"

"I'm sorry, but this is how it has to be, my friend." I turn away and walk across her porch. This is truly difficult for me, too.

"Wait!" she calls out.

"What?" I turn around and glare.

"What about your clothes in the guest bedroom closet?"

"I don't need them. Goodbye won't be forever, I promise."

"Okay." She sniffles. "At least, call me sometime."

"I will." I turn away and walk to my car. I won't look back again lest I change my mind. I will go back to Claire's tonight. Then tomorrow I will look for my own place to live. That's all that makes sense. I can't be homeless forever and crashing in beds that aren't mine. *No, for once*, I tell myself, *do the right thing!*

I am back at Claire's house by nine p.m. On my way over, I stopped at a restaurant and ordered a huge salad for supper, deciding to lose another ten pounds before my cosmetic procedure. Why pay for a younger-looking face if my body looks like hell? No, I must be disciplined in my actions, trusting God I am on the right path.

Does that mean I've become a Buddhist?

Claire opens the door for me before I get the chance.

"Mama, where have you been? I've been worried sick."

"I went to see Ellie Simpson." I tromp into the kitchen and deposit my purse on the bar. "And I broke up with Lorene."

Claire slumps in the barstool. "I won't touch that one."

I smile, lean over the bar, and pat my daughter's hand. "That's so sweet, honey. You've just made my day. How is Ted?"

"He's out for the night, sound asleep." She smacks her lips.

"Did you ask him if he was cheating on you?" I inquire.

"I don't think he was guilty of adultery yesterday," she says.

That doesn't make him innocent, I note to myself.

"Okay, but if lipstick shows up on his shirt again, you'd better have that conversation. Don't put up with infidelity. You can make it on your own if you have to. Marriage is a commitment, honey."

"I know." Claire nods. "Do you want to play some cards?"

"What kind?"

"Rummy." She pulls out a pack from the drawer and deals us a hand. I think mindless games are a good way to escape reality.

20

Saturday, May 13

THE SUN IS A DIAMOND in the sky this morning. I've seldom seen such a deep blue swath of atmosphere covering our space. The air is cool and fresh and I think our Creator is smiling on Tennessee.

I am standing on Claire's front porch watching bluebirds twitter from branch to branch in a large oak with expansive branches like wings. I am reminded that angels look down on us and wonder why we create so much trouble when all God wants is peace on earth.

"A penny for your thoughts?" Claire utters as she joins me.

"Oh, I don't know. Guess I'm in a poetic mood."

"Ted is up and hungry. He wants pancakes."

I look at my daughter. "I'm trying to lose a few pounds."

"Okay, you can have one of Ted's health shakes. We're having pancakes slathered in Maple syrup with crisp bacon. Your choice."

"You are such a tease." I get up and follow her inside the house.

Ted is slumped at the breakfast bar looking like he was in a barfight instead of an automobile accident. "Good morning, Ted."

"Mornin', Mama."

I love that he calls me that and not Dorothy.

"How did the accident happen?" I ask.

"A teen driving a pickup was texting his girlfriend," Ted sourly replies. "They will never make it as a couple."

"Why not?" I pour myself a cup of Joe and add cream.

"He died." Ted glares at Claire.

She places her hand over his and says, "I'm glad it wasn't you, Ted. I'm sorry for the boy, but you belong to this family. I love you."

I am moved by Claire's confession. I've not heard her declare her feelings so succinctly to Theodore in some years. Maybe this fear of losing one another will have an impact on their relationship. Two people bound together in a marriage should not remain silent.

I think of Tom. I never told him that I loved him. Maybe I did not want to admit the truth to myself. Perhaps, I am guilty of adultery in my thoughts, and Arthur is shaking his finger at me. *Shame, shame.*

Doesn't matter, I'll probably never see Tom again.

"Mama. Did you decide on pancakes?"

I glance up at my daughter. *Huh?*

"Pancakes or a health shake?"

"Uh, I'll have what you're having," I say.

She chuckles. "I swear, you are in a mood this morning."

Ted pounds the bar with his good hand. "Wife! Food!"

I leap to the task. "I'll take care of the bacon."

Within fifteen minutes, we are gorging on Aunt Jemima Pancakes. As promised, it's the best food I've had all day, although my first.

"That was mighty good, Claire." Ted slobbers as he swipes his sticky lips with a hand. He isn't aging well. Too chubby, but I don't think he cares. He'll never reclaim the image he had when he married my daughter. Then, after thirty-two years, who does?

I have a stab of guilt. Who am I to be critical of others? I have wrinkles galore. I have yet to tell Claire about my cosmetic surgery.

Ted goes back to bed while I help Claire tidy the kitchen. She doesn't clean the house from top to bottom anymore since Ted hired a maid to come twice a week. I wonder sometimes if she's bored.

We are having our second round of coffees on the back patio when Claire asks, "When are you going to view property?"

"I have time today if I can get a real estate guide," I reply, then Google on my phone companies in the Brentwood area. Almost instantly, a number of brand names appear on my screen. All I need to do is select the CALL button to get an agent on the phone.

"Did you get a hit?" Claire asks, and I think of the bullet I almost took when I was kidnapped last year.

"I'm dialing now. Shush!" I wait for a real person to answer. No such luck; I get a voicemail requesting I leave a message, so I will.

"Nobody there?" Claire stretches out on the lounge chair, her long legs tanning beautifully. She is a younger version of me, except she has red hair and mine is—well, gray, with some red highlights.

"Somebody is hungry enough to call me back, trust me."

My phone jingles.

"There!" I chime in with a jolly-O hello.

Then I sit up and my smile fades into a frown. "What?"

Claire alerts to my emotional display. *What?*

I shake my head, trying to make sense of what Lorene is telling me. "Stop! One word at a time, Lorene! Start over again."

Claire is seated upright in the lounge chair, trying to put together what I am hearing at the other end of this phone conversation.

Finally, Lorene gets through with her tale of woe and I end the call. "I need to go back to Columbia. A friend has died."

"What friend?" Claire stands and extends a hand to help me up from my chair. I am wobbly and upset and angry all at once.

"It's my young friend, Zoey Jackson."

"The one in college you support?"

I nod my head, tears clouding my vision.

"What about her?" Claire asks.

"She committed suicide."

"Why?"

"That's what I want to know, and you can bet your last dollar she had help." I think of the big black man in Ellie's barn. "The Russian Mafia is not through with any of us that had anything to do with the take down of four state bosses. I'm sure this is payback time."

I head for the backdoor and open it.

"Wait, Mama! What are you going to do?"

I blink tears and spurt, "Something, that's for damn sure!"

21

I DRIVE TOO FAST TOWARD Columbia, ignoring the traffic and the road signs. If a cop stops me for speeding, I will lie. I don't care that I am a Methodist. I am on a mission to right a wrong. A *deadly* wrong.

I drive straight to the morgue to speak with Lorene's daughter-in-law, Dr. Cynthia Perkins. The odor of formaldehyde greets me as I exit the elevator in the basement of the antiquated building that houses the CSI unit. I know where I am going, so I ask no one for help. The staff is too busy to notice me or care about why I am here.

I push open the door to Cyn's office without knocking.

She looks up, stunned. "Mrs. Powell, what are you doing here?"

"Have you processed Zoey Jackson's body yet?"

She stands up, a little wobbly. I note the dark circles rimming her beautiful cinnamon-colored eyes, as big as half dollars—not that I've seen many of the coins floating around in the financial market.

"She's in the cooler. I'm waiting for her father to identify her."

"The one in prison?" I park my purse on an empty chair and plant my butt in another. I am too old to deal with this kind of trauma.

Cyn closes the door and trundles back down at her desk.

"Who is Zoey to you?" she inquires.

"It's a long story—I've taken a liking to her in the past few years and pay her tuition in college." I am suddenly too warm and panicky.

Cyn's gaze squeezes. "Are you okay, Mrs. Powell?"

"No, Dr. Perkins, I will never be all right again. Zoey did not commit suicide. The idea is not built into her psyche. She had a future planned and I was helping her accomplish her dreams."

"From all appearances, Detective Chico thinks her death was."

I open my mouth then shut it. Then I get up and turn around.

"Where are you going?" Cyn asks.

I turn around and face the coroner.

"To see Zoey's body, where is she?"

Cyn walks over and opens the door for me.

"I'll need to go with you."

I look at her, eye to eye. "Thank you."

But I was going to the cold storage unit with or without her. I know where it's located. My Arthur was lying dead in there a few years ago. We march down the hallway like we're sisters-in-hood.

Her assistant Gordy—officially Dr. Gordon Mills—is examining Zoey's naked body. Seeing her like that gives me a profound pause.

Dear God, what are you thinking? Letting someone kill her like this? When she's barely twenty-one and will graduate as a nurse soon?

But God doesn't answer me. He's like that sometimes. He lets the bad people get away with the unthinkable, then tells me not to judge them, that they will get what's coming to them in the Afterlife.

But I think like Tom. I want to help with their judgment.

* * *

Detective Galena Chico is seated in Captain Marilyn Colbert's office discussing Zoey Jackson's death. Every detail points to a suicide. She was found in her boyfriend's bedroom overdosed with cocaine. And the vial was in her right hand. Should be a shut-and-closed case.

"Tell me, Detective . . ." Marilyn leans forward, forearms resting on the desk, "what makes you believe Zoey did not commit suicide?"

"Testimonies of friends," Galena replies, sipping on a vanilla latte.

The Columbia Police Department had set up a fancy coffee bar in the atrium for its officers and staff instead of paying megabucks out to the Coffee Call delivery service. A minimal charge was appreciated.

Weary to the bone from a sleepless night, Galena shifts in the chair and adds, "True, Zoey's ex-boyfriend sold drugs. But she broke up with him a month ago. Everyone I've interviewed at the Community College says she was straight, never took anything illegal."

"Okay, but if it looks like a duck, and waddles like a duck . . ."

"Perceptions can be skewed," Galena argues as she leans forward and her latte sloshes, quickly licking up the fallen liquid with a napkin.

"Don't worry about the floor, maid comes tonight," the captain says, pondering over Galena's statement. "Okay, so it's a homicide."

Galena nods. "That's what I think. But who took her life?"

"Maybe the boyfriend—maybe Zoey knew too much about his business," Marilyn offers. "Maybe, his boss ordered the hit."

Galena nods again. "Is this homicide connected to the murders three years ago?" She refers to the deaths of Arthur Powell, Crawford Perkins, and Clyde Willems. "Is the Russian Mafia involved?"

"I don't know." Marilyn replies. "I'd have to read more closely the details of your report again. Was Zoey ever involved with them?"

"Yes, she kept the books on funds received from a prostitute ring operating in Nashville," Galena replies. "She found local girls needing cash to pimp for them. Sonja Berioski was her boss."

"How did she get off scot-free?"

"She ratted on them." But there had been consequences.

"I recall when that operation was taken down in Nashville," Marilyn reveals. "Some lawyer's client rolled on them."

"Dorothy Powell's son-in-law, Attorney Theodore Burkes."

"Well, that would certainly put Zoey in the Mafia's headlights."

"Everything they do is about loyalty. And payback," Galena says.

"So, it appears. But where do we begin unravelling this difficult series of murders that appear to be connected?"

"I don't know. Should I call someone at TBI?" Galena asks.

The Tennessee Bureau of Investigations was the equivalent of the FBI but operated withing the borders of the state. They often cooperated with the Central Intelligence agencies in Washington, DC.

"Might as well. And send a courier over with the reports and notes on the death of our two old guys from three years ago."

After Galena left the building, she dialed a familiar number. An agent she knew personally that might assist with this investigation.

* * *

Twenty minutes later, I am still at the morgue with Dr. Cynthia Perkins when my cell phone vibrates in my purse.

"Excuse me, Dr. Perkins. I need to take this call."

I step out of the room where the dead are kept. "Hello."

"Mrs. Powell?"

"All day long," I reply.

"Where are you?"

"Who are you?" I ask in return.
"Detective Chico. Are you busy?"
"I was, but I'm not now. What do you want?"
"Can you come over to my office now?"
"Sure, I'm already in Columbia," I reply.

As much as I've tried to leave this town, something keeps dragging me back. I think ultimately that it's Crystal Creek. The waterway seems to flow all the way to Nashville, and I keep swimming back like a top-notch athlete diving into trouble. Where is it taking me now?

22

I PHONE LORENE WHILE driving over to the precinct where Detective Lloyd Peters formerly had his office. That was before he was murdered by an assassin last November who is possibly trying to kill me. "What are you doing right now, friend?" I ask her.

"Dorothy! Are you in town?"

"Yes, Lorene. Detective Chico wants to talk to me."

"That can't be good."

I hear a sigh in her voice and know she's stressed over Zoey Jackson's presumed suicide. I am convinced that's not possible.

"Are you feeling any better?" I inquire.

"No, I'm sick to my soul over Zoey's death," she tells me. "Such a beautiful life snuffed out so suddenly. I can't believe she committed suicide." Lorene sniffles and I offer up a quick prayer for her.

"She didn't kill herself, Lorene. Someone took her life."

"That's not what the morning paper said."

"I don't care about fake news!" I explode a little too brilliantly. "Sorry, I've got my britches in a twist over her murder."

"*Murder?* Who said anything about murder?"

"I did, Lorene. And I'm betting that Detective Chico feels the same way." I pull up to the precinct and park in the GUEST slot.

"I tried calling earlier but you didn't answer your cell phone."

"I was at the morgue viewing Zoey's body," I answer as I get out of my BMW and lock up. "She looked like an angel, so beautiful."

Lorene sniffles again. "Are you spending the night with me?"

I chuckle. "Did you forget we're divorced?"

"Don't be silly, you are my best friend."

I hear a bright note in her voice. "Why don't we discuss our break-up over lunch? About noon, at Coffee Call?"

"Sure. I need to shower and wake up Graham."

"Graham is there—has he moved in with you?"

"Last night," Lorene replies. "His stuff is in storage."

"Cynthia never mentioned anything to me about that."

"It was a spur-of-the-moment decision."

I let the matter drop; not important in light of what's happened.

"Just because I have permanent guests does not mean you can't spend the night. Dorothy. My king-size bed will accommodate at least three people." She is bent on convincing me to cancel our divorce.

"Three? Are we inviting a gentleman to join us?" I tease.

"Be serious!" she spurts, and I imagine her embarrassment.

"Okay, honey, I'll think about a sleepover. See you at lunch."

I end the call and walk into the building. Officer Jake is manning the front desk. I raise my arms. "No weapons, Officer, I'm here to see Detective Chico. Call up if you wish, or I can just elevate myself."

He chuckles. "You are too much, Dorothy."

I see that gleam in his younger eyes. He wants a date with me. He thinks I'm easy because I am old. And he's probably heard rumors that the former Senior Citizen Center manager was sweet on me.

Ah, I think, *what he doesn't know doesn't hurt me.*

Chico also has her britches in a twist. She's all over her male secretary as she views his computer and fusses about her afternoon appointments. "Blake! I'm not two people. Cancel the mayor."

"The mayor? You're certain." His limber fingers lift from the keyboard. "He might not like it—but, uh, you are the boss."

Chico looks up. "Oh. You. I almost forgot."

I shrug. Some people like me; others don't.

"Get my appointments straight, Blake, or you're fired."

"Yes, ma'am." He dives into the work before him.

"If this is an inconvenient time, I can come back tomorrow," I tell the beautiful Latino detective as I enter her office and sit down.

"No." She slams the door. "Now is better."

I sit stiffly, not wanting her on my bad side today.

"Hard to get reliable help these days—I need to ask you a few questions." She drops in her chair at the desk, dark curls tumbling into her face as the hair clasp at the back of her head snaps. "Just like the rest of my day!" She brushes away the curls so she can see me.

"Maybe you should take a moment to chill out," I offer some advice, but the frown on her face tells me it is not appreciated.

"Or, forget I'm here." I get up to leave.

"Sit, Mrs. Powell."

I pause in my tracks. It's more of a command, so I do. I turn around and glare at her. "Am I under arrest, Detective Chico? Have I done something illegal?" I am not in the best of moods, either.

All the oomph seems to slide out of the detective. "I'm sorry, I'm taking my frustration out of you. And probably Blake, too."

I nod. She's right and I won't argue as I sit down.

"Why am I here, Detective Chico?"

"I met with Captain Colbert earlier today. M.E. Dr. Perkins phoned and said you stopped by the morgue. So, I know you've heard about Zoey Jackson's death. I understand you were close to her."

No comment. That's not a crime.

"Captain Colbert and I believe these recent attempts on your life may be related to the murders that occurred here three years ago," she reveals. Manicured nails, though cut short, rest on her desk.

"I've said that all along, but no one seems to listen."

"I'm listening and so is Captain Colbert. Tell me what you think." Her gaze metaphorically pins me to the wall.

"What I think?" I inwardly smile. "Am I on your team now?"

No answer, so I move on.

"Well, I think the black guy I saw in Ellie Simpson's barn is the same person that tried to blow up Lorene Perkin's house. He must have trailed us over to Ellie's late Wednesday afternoon on May 10th then returned to her house to set the stage for a gas-range explosion.

"If Lorene's son Sam had not discovered the gas-range leak Thursday morning, both Lorene and I would be toast."

I let that thought settle into Chico's smart brain.

"Zoey's death is payback, Detective. The Russian Mafia."

Chico nods; thinks about what I've said. Then she leans forward and lays a bombshell on me, "You should be in Protective Custody."

What? I realize it was a thought and not verbal. Then I think if Thomas Kessler can guard me again, it might not be so bad.

"Mrs. Powell? Are you willing to go into Protective Custody?"

"No. I won't give up my life to run from the bad guys." I think maybe I should purchase a pistol and visit the shooting range.

Chico sits back, tilts her fancy office chair back, and laces her long fingers over her slender belly—which reminds me mine isn't, and that I have a scheduled facelift and haven't yet told my daughter about it.

"Okay," she says. "I thought I'd offer."

I let a couple of seconds slip by, hoping I've made the right decision. I do not have nine lives like the proverbial cat. Plus, I'm not as brave as I let on. But to reinvent my life at my age? No way.

"I guess we're finished here," Chico says.

"One more question. When will Zoey Jackson's body be released for burial?" I feel planning her funeral is my responsibility since her father is serving time in the penitentiary and she has no one else.

"Not sure when her father will be brought over to the morgue to identify her," she replies. "Why? Are you related to Zoey?"

"No, but I've been financially supporting Zoey while she attends college ever since my husband Arthur's death. She was studying to be a nurse. There is no way she would have killed herself."

"So, no suicide." Chico taps her pen on her desktop.

"Nope. Pure murder staged to look like a suicide."

"I agree," Chico said. "Don't go far, I'll be in touch."

"Okay." I gather my purse to leave.

Chico walks me through the front office to the door.

"Watch your back, Mrs. Powell."

I turn around and smile. "You, too, Detective Chico."

23

COFFEE CALL IS BECKONING to me as I step through the door. Chicory and pastry odors overwhelm my tastebuds and I suspect I am capable of eating enough for three people. But I will refrain.

Lorene spots me and waves me over.

I buzz past a server and sit down across from my best friend at a glass-top table for two. There's only floor space for my big purse.

"Have you been waiting long?" I lock eyes with Lorene.

"Fifteen minutes tops." She sniffles.

"You are still upset about Zoey's death," I conclude.

"That, and I'm catching a spring cold."

"It's too late for Spring, dear. A summer cold is much worse."

"Bearer of bad news!" she gushes while frowning.

"Yeah . . . that's me." I lean back in my uncomfortable straight chair and inhale deeply. "Chico wants me in a Protection program."

"Detective Chico?" Lorene alights to the news.

"Well, she's not employed by the clothing company." I giggle. "And she never wears jewelry." I flatten my hands on the table.

A male with a crooked nose stands over us. I look up, amazed at his height. I question if I'm too nosy if I ask him how he broke it.

"I know, I'm six eight, ladies. Should be playing on our high school basketball team," he explains. "But I got kicked off recently for bad behavior. And . . . part of my punishment is to serve others."

His badge has his name spelled JON. His smile is crooked like his nose, but he has an interesting face in a rugged sort of way.

"That was, uh, a mouthful," Lorene reacts, seeing I'm about to put my foot in my nosy mouth and embarrass the both of us.

"And *this* is the only way you can find to serve others? Coffee and pastries?" I cannot help myself. "What about Community Service?"

He shifts his lanky body from one foot to the other—his huge feet clad in an expensive pair of sports tennis shoes. Eyes a strange color of yellow mud, he makes me think of a sleek monster.

I know . . . I'm being judgmental again.

"I could do Community Service." Tall-and-Lanky yanks his neck to one side and it cracks like a popsicle stick. "But I like coffee."

"Me, too." I grab the laminated menu and decide on a deluxe vanilla-caramel latte with three shots of expresso, extra whip cream, with chocolate drizzle. "Number 4," I tell Jon. *Big Jon.*

"I'll have that, too, for starters," Lorene says. "But I want your Big Burger with Everything-But-The-Kitchen-Sink."

"You, Miss?" His lazy hazel eyes stare down at me like a bear.

He called me "Miss" and I feel giddy. An old woman like myself absorbs compliments like a paper towel soaking up liquid.

"You want the burger, too?" Jon mutters, rolling a wad of gum around in his mouth as he cracks his neck again.

"Bring it on, Jon!" I snap a napkin in my lap.

After he jaunts away like the athlete he is, Lorene leans across the table. "He's cute, sort of. Your cheeks are flushed like a teenager's."

I wave the napkin like a fan to cool my jets. "I still have feelings, Lorene. I'm not stone yet, and I'm not cold in the grave . . . so . . ."

"So, I wish I'd never commented."

We glare at one another. Friends are like that. They can get so aggravated at one another a fight might break out. Then reality sets in. Friends are hard to come by. It takes years to meld with someone.

"Which reminds me . . ." I chime in, "are we playing Canasta on Friday with the girls?" Making plans makes me feel safer.

"Does the sun come out every morning?"

"Don't be cute, I might slap you."

"Let's not fight. I don't want a divorce."

The couple seated at the table next to us give us *that* look. *Are they gay? Getting a divorce? Who would've thought in Columbia?*

I laugh so hard I think I'm going to faint.

"What is so funny, Dorothy?"

"Nothing. Everything. Let's don't talk; just drink and eat."

"Like this is the last meal we will ever have," she says.

I won't give that statement credence. Jon is back in ten minutes with our coffee orders. "Thank you." I smile sweetly as I look up.

"Burgers will be up in fifteen." He slip-slides away in those expensive tennis shoes as younger women ogle him. I bet he gets a lot of tips. More than Community Service would pay," Lorene says. "I bet he doesn't even drink coffee. He's more the Sports Drink kind."

"It's none of our business anyhow," I decide.

"Okay, toots!" Lorene pounds the table with her coffee mug. "Tell me what Detective Chico had to say."

I go through the whole spiel as I recall our latest conversation. "Bottom line, she agrees with me that Zoey Jackson was murdered."

"What else did you tell her?"

"That I believed your gas leak was a murder attempt on us."

"No wonder she wants you in Protective Custody."

A pause as we assess our situation.

"Changing the subject, Dorothy, will you spend the night?"

Our neighbors at the next table turn their heads on us as they process Lorene's statement. I only shake my head. After contemplating Lorene's question, I say, "No, I need to go home and check on Ted when we're done here." I realize she doesn't know about his accident.

"Why? What's wrong with Ted?"

The next fifteen minutes are devoted to a replay of Claire's dramatic speech in thinking Ted was cheating on her with a younger woman. The red lipstick on his shirt collar, and the phone call that came the next morning, put her in a mood. All drama, drama, drama.

"That's awful!" Lorene exclaims. "She should divorce him."

"Come on now, where is your faith in humanity? Turns out Claire's worry was a false alarm; Ted was not cheating on her."

"Thank God for good endings."

"Well, he's pretty banged up," I note. "And his car is totaled."

"He had a wreck in that beautiful Mercedes Benz?"

"Yep, but he's fine, and he has good insurance."

"Maybe he wrecked because he was talking to his Sweetie," Lorene suggests. She's seen too many soap operas over the decades.

"Flesh will heal but emotions sometimes don't," she adds.

I think of our husbands, how we lost them on the same day. If we could go back and do something different, would they still be alive?

Those are questions for the angels to ask God. No human can understand the awfulness of Fate. Even though God loves all of us.

We finish our burgers and leave the bistro together. I walk Lorene to her car. "I'll come over Thursday night and stay with you."

"Oh, good! Then we can ride to the Senior Citizen Center together for lunch and cards." She uses the fob to get in her Tesla.

"Okay, it's a date, honey!" I say loudly, for the benefit of the couple leaving the coffee shop. The ones that sat at the table next to us. I am so full of foolishness today I could kick myself.

"Call me," Lorene says as she gets in her car.

I wave goodbye but she doesn't drive away. The passenger window comes down. "Is that your car driving past?" She points to my red BMW. The top is rolled back and the driver looks happy.

"Yeah, but that isn't me driving!" I exclaim.

24

"**WHAT DO YOU WANT** to do now?" Lorene glares at me.

"Now that I don't have a car?" I almost laugh at the situation. How could anybody be so unlucky? "Take me to the police station."

"Now?" Lorene pulls back into her parking space and the motor idles. "It may be too early to file a Missing Vehicle Report."

I park my hands on my bony hips, peering at her and disgusted with the situation. How can anyone get carjacked on court square?

"Okay—whatever you say," Lorene mutters and motions for me to climb in her Tesla. "I won't argue with a disgruntled old woman."

I fill the passenger seat and repress angry tears.

Lorene backs out in the street again and we drive a few blocks to the police station where Captain Marilyn Colbert has an office.

She pulls into a parking space for guests. Again, the motor idles.

"You don't have to wait for me, Lorene."

"Why not?" She rolls her lime-colored eyes in thought.

"When I'm finished here, I'll either rent a car or call Claire to come and get me." I open the passenger door and nearly fall out.

Then with composure, lean into the car to say one more thing.

"What?" Lorene wonders.

"Always lock your car, even when you think it is safe," I advise.

"Even in the bright daylight in front of the courthouse?"

"Let the evidence speak for itself." I slam the door and walk into the station, not looking back as I hear Lorene drive away.

A rookie officer is at the admission desk. He glares at me.

I wonder if I have coffee split down my blouse.

"How may I help you, Mrs. Powell?"

Huh? "Do I know you, uh, Officer?" I ask the young cop with carrot-colored hair that sticks straight up and eyes the color of mud.

"Everyone knows you, Mrs. Powell? How may we help you?"

We? It's as if the whole town is trying to watch my back. I might as well wear a sign: BORN FOR TROUBLE. I sigh, realizing Arthur might turn over in his grave if Jesus tells him I'm the talk of the town.

Harold is his name—it's on his nametag.

"I need to file a Missing Vehicle Report," I tell him.

He jacks a thumb over his left shoulder. "Go through that door and ask somebody at the counter. They will help you."

"Thank you, Harold. You have been very helpful."

I hold my head up high, march ten paces across the tile floor, and push open the door with the insignia CLERK OF COURT.

No one stands at the counter as if ready to help me.

"Hello!" I make myself known and wait.

No one comes to the counter.

I wait a couple of minutes.

No one comes.

"I NEED HELP!" I call out loudly.

Boy, does that get everyone's attention! Four people in police uniforms exit two doors behind the counter and stare at me.

"Are you injured?" one of the two female officers asks.

"No, I need help in filling out a Missing Vehicle Report."

"False alarm!" she calls out. The other three disappear through the doors and I have to wonder if coffee and snacks are back there.

The officer slaps a form in my hand and points to the door to my right. "Go in there. Sit down, fill out the report, then bring it back."

Her gaze is poignant, and I suspect she recognizes me.

"Hey! You're Dorothy Powell!" She grins like I'm her friend.

"Yes, I am." I will try not to be cute and get myself arrested.

"Captain Colbert is looking for you."

"She is?" This is a new wrinkle in the day that needs ironing out.

"You ought 'a go on up to the captain's office and see what she wants," Officer Miller says. "Come back later and finish your report."

"All right." I lay the form on the counter and exit the office.

The elevator is down a short hallway. I ride up to the fourth floor and find the office door marked CAPTAIN MARILYN COLBERT.

The door comes open before I have a chance to politely knock.

"Mrs. Powell!"

My name is the same as the last time I checked.

"Were you looking for me?" I gingerly inquire.

"Yes, Detective Chico told me you declined Protective Services." She crooks a finger, signaling for me to come inside her office.

I trail her past the secretary at the computer and enter her private domain. It's a larger space than Chico's. I linger for instructions.

"Have a seat, Mrs. Powell."

Always obedient to the police, I sit down in the only vacant chair in the office then place my oversized purse on the floor beside me.

"Why don't you accept police protection?" she queries.

I contemplate my answer. The middle-aged woman's irises are as black as her silky skin, but her warm smile lightens everything about her persona. She's likable, professionally sharp, and puts me at ease.

"Look. I'm old, Captain Colbert, and I just want to live my life without worrying every second that somebody is trying to kill me."

"But someone is bent on taking your life," she counters.

"I know. But God is on my side." I'm concrete on this point.

"What if He's busy sometimes?"

I know she's teasing but I respond anyhow. "Then I'll go to Heaven to be with my deceased husband Arthur." Plain and simple.

The captain turns around and grabs a manila folder from the credenza; opens it on her desk upside down for me to view.

"Is this the man you saw in Ellie Simpson's barn not long ago?" she queries, then waits for me to take a closer look.

I pull the picture closer. "Yes, that's him. Who is he?"

"A very bad man with a lot of people working with him."

"Okay, is he the one that tried to blow up Lorene Perkins' house?"

"No proof he did, but someone he hired may have," she reasons. "Dom is the top man for the Russian Mafia working out of Nashville."

"Why is this Dom character interested in me?" I'm puzzled over my importance to so sophisticated a criminal organization.

"We don't actually know, but we suspect it's more than payback for your involvement with exposing the Mafia bosses in four states last fall," she replies. "You met the Kentucky boss in a snowstorm."

We again. Like a conspiracy. The Mafia assassin, Mark Hagen, kidnapped me last fall and took me to a cabin outside of Crossville during a snowstorm. I was interrogated by Leonard Stoldt. A combined task force from the Tennessee Bureau of Investigations and the Central Intelligence Agency assaulted the cabin with bullets flying every which way in an effort to save me. Stoldt and Hagen died. And Clint Howard, a.k.a. Thomas Kessler, took a bullet for me.

"Take a guess then." I refer to the reason I am hunted like prey.

"You realize this is a need-to-know question."

I nod. I'm not stupid. I've done my share of snooping.

She continues, "Okay, this is just a guess, you understand."

Her gaze pins me to my seat and I feel like I'm under a microscope lens. "I understand. I promise not to repeat anything you say."

The smile tucked in her expression suggests she doesn't believe me. "Scouts honor," I add with gusto. "I mean Girl Scouts honor."

Captain Colbert leans across her desk toward me.

I wait with anticipation.

"Where is the library book with the coded words?" She erects her stout figure and straightens her shoulders, thick lips in a twist.

The book Clyde Willems gave Arthur for his birthday?

She senses my hesitancy.

"The one you and the CIA agent located with codes that led to the identification of four Mafia bosses," she clarifies.

"I know which book!" I reply, probably a little too harshly. "What does *that* book have to do with the bad guys wanting me dead now?"

The captain taps her pen on her large calendar. "That's where the mystery comes in, Mrs. Powell. It makes no sense."

I nod in agreement, feeling a bit out of my element. I want to get this interview over with and locate my beautiful, stolen, red BMW.

"Okay . . ." I smack my lips. "Let's just say the book contains more codes the CIA missed the first time." I shrug. "In that case, the Mafia may think I know something that will hurt them again."

"Okay. . . that's an excellent point."

"But, Captain Colbert, I don't have the book anymore."

"Neither does the CIA," she informs me.

What? I am startled by that remark.

"Are you in touch with Agent Thomas Kessler?"

"No, I presume he died from his bullet wound."

It's a little white lie. Surely, Tom was the person who sent me the Christmas card postmarked from Moscow, Russia.

"What do the CIA gurus think?"

Captain Colbert appears flustered.

"I know—it's a need-to-know, so you don't have to tell me," I say to ease her apparent frustration. "But you want to tell me."

"Agent Kessler isn't dead, but he's missing," she reveals.

"Oh." *Kidnapped or ran away?*

Lip-locked in a conversation that has no place else to go, I do not have a response. Yet, I am thrilled to finally have confirmation that Tom lives another day. Still, I worry the Russian thugs have him.

Colbert's desk phone rings and shatters the silence.

"Excuse me." She spins in her chair toward the wall. "Yes?"

I clasp my hands while waiting to be dismissed.

"She's here, in my office." Captain Colbert swivels around in her ergonomic chair and gazes at me, her expression growing dark.

"Okay, I will tell her."

The sound of the phone set in its jacket nearly startles me.

"What has happened now? Is Lorene Perkins all right?"

"They found your car. The officer on the crash scene—"

"Wait! What crash scene?" I am standing before I realize it.

"You have a red BMW?" She repeats the car tag number.

"Yes, I do. Did you catch the guy that stole it?"

"We got him. Only he did not survive the crash. Officer James clocked him at one-hundred miles an hour on the interstate before he rolled your BMW over and landed in a ditch. It exploded on the spot."

My car exploded? My mouth hangs open like a thirsty dog. If my tongue could flap, it would. I am trembling and feel badly for the thief.

"Mrs. Powell, from what Officer James could see when the flames died down, your brake line had been cut," Colbert explains.

I drop in the chair like a lead balloon. "Someone cut my brake line?" I am rethinking Detective Chico's offer for Protective Services.

25

CLAIRE IS AT THE Columbia Police Station an hour-and-a-half after I called her. I'm seated in the vaulted atrium while waiting her arrival. When I spot her Buick outside, I exit the station and jam myself into the passenger seat. My great-granddaughter June's head leans between the two front seats. "GG? Are you in trouble again?" she whispers.

I glance back and see little hands cupped around her rosebud lips as if MGM cannot hear her question. I used to think those letters stood for a movie company. Not anymore. GG for "Great Grandmother" and MGM for "My Grand Mother." I'm not in the mood for teasing.

"Are you okay, Mama?" Claire notes my frown.

Thank God, Claire speaks ordinary English.

"I've had better days." I shrug as the V-6 motor idles.

Claire backs out of the parking space and turns toward I-65, the best route to take us to her house. "Are you going to tell me what happened—how you ended up stranded at the Police Station?"

"I will, but not now. We'll talk about it when we get home."

I am beginning to think of Claire's house as my home. I don't want to be a burden to Theodore and my sweet daughter, but honest to goodness, I have not had the time to find my own place. Every time I think I have a day to look at properties, another disaster occurs.

We ride in silence over paved roads that never seem to end.

Every time June opens her mouth, Claire calls out, "Not now, June." So, she sits back in her car seat, plugs in her earbuds, and listens to God-knows-what kind of music. This new generation is a puzzle.

"Is Ted home?" He'd wrecked his Mercedes late last week. He blames the young guy using his phone while driving. I don't think the insurance adjuster has worked out all the details of payout yet.

"No, a coworker took him to the office."

Claire parks her Buick in the driveway and we get out. June knows how to unbuckle the seatbelt so she lands on the concrete like a long-range jumper. Inside the house, Claire drops her purse on the kitchen counter then adds water to the KEURIG Coffeemaker.

Then looks at me. "Flavored or regular coffee?"

"Uh, regular." I need caffeine. Life for me is already flavored.

June sits on the sofa, still fiddling with her iPhone. I think Dr. Google must know the answer to every question in the universe. I wonder why children even need to attend school. Another world.

Claire hands me my cup across the bar.

"The coffee smells wonderful." I take a sip and sigh.

She leans over the counter, close to my face. "Mama, you know I love you very much. Right?" She sips her coffee heavy with cream.

"I know." I touch her sweet face. "I love you, too."

"But June has a point about you getting into too much trouble."

My teeth clench at the remark. "Don't you dare say 'for my age'!"

Claire's chuckle forces her to spit coffee on the bar. "Sorry." She quickly mops up the liquid with a paper towel she ripped from its rack.

"I don't know what to say, Claire. Trouble chases me." I never look for it. Who wants trouble? Not me. I want peace and quiet.

"I just want a normal mother," she quips.

"I wish I could deliver that to you, sweetheart, but I'm not that."

It's a conclusion I have reached following Arthur's death. I always did exactly as he asked me. I never questioned his authority to choose what was best for us. He was the head of our household. And I loved him very much. Even more, I respected him. But now that he's gone . . . now that I'm *alone*. I have to find a way to live my life.

"Dr. Sharra phoned me looking for you."

"He did." I have not told Claire I have a facelift scheduled.

"Who is this doctor? Do you have cancer?"

I spew out my coffee and laugh hard.

"Mama! What is going on?"

I grasp Claire's hand. "I don't have cancer, I have wrinkles."

June calls out, "I told you GG was crazy."

"What kind of doctor is Sharra?" Claire asks again, as serious as a bullet aimed at my heart. I can tell she's not up to a lie.

"Lyle Sharra is a cosmetic surgeon. I have a procedure scheduled for Friday, June 2nd in Columbia. I'm straightening my face."

June tosses her phone. "Can I go outside and play now?"

"Sure, but don't go out in the street. And stay in the backyard. Be careful not to fall off the playset," Claire issues instructions.

June parks a small hand on one hip, so cute I want to grab her up and smother her with kisses. "MGM, you know me better."

Then she runs out the back door.

"I'm tired, Claire. I think I'll go and lie down."

"Okay, Mama. But when you wake up from a nap, I want to know how you ended up at the Police Station without your vehicle."

"I'll explain, I promise," I say then trudge through the den and down the hall to the guest bedroom like a nomad moving through a sandstorm. Life just keeps on throwing BS at me. I won't say it.

After all, I am a good Methodist. Sometimes.

* * *

Three hours passed before I woke up. The moon hangs in a tree in Claire's front yard, twinkling like a lantern through its oak leaves. I have no idea what time it is, nor do I care. My stomach grumbles, so I suspect I have missed supper. I open the door to the guest bedroom and peek into the hallway. No sign of life. No noises, except for a coo-coo clock in the kitchen that counts off the hours. I stand there like a first grader and mentally count the number of crows.

8 p.m. It's too early for Claire and Ted to be in bed so I wonder where they are. Never mind, I can make my own sandwich. I know my way around Claire's kitchen. After I've eaten and had a glass of cold milk, I open the backdoor to the patio. There, they sit. Claire and Ted.

Only they are not holding hands. No. Or hugging each other like empty-nesters ought to do. They are having a rather belligerent argument—only in a whispering fashion. I presume so neighbors won't hear them. I am not a neighbor. So, I will listen with caution.

"I can't believe you suspected me of having an affair, Claire."

"What about the lipstick on your shirt?" Claire asks him. "It's happened on more than one occasion in the past two months."

Ted rears back and looks at his wife. "I can't help it if women like me, Claire. We often have drinks, and they lean on me for support."

"You take your female clients out to dinner, wine and dine them until they are drunk? Then what? A little attention feels good?"

"That's mean!" Ted barks, his expression distorted.

It's time I make myself known before a fight breaks out.

I clear my throat. "Am I interrupting something?"

Two heads turn my way, startled by my presence.

I throw a hand. "I heard, my dears." I walk out on the patio and drag up a chair. "This discussion is utter foolishness. Why would either of you let another human being come between you? You have two healthy children and two grands that adore you. God loves you both."

Claire scoots her chair away from the table and stands up.

"Mama, stay out of this."

Ted haughtily looks at me. I know he agrees.

I plop down in the chair ready to give advice.

"Not now, Mama!" Claire cautions.

"I'll have my say and leave the battle to you," I tell her with no other options on the table. "Love is kind; it has a way of forgiving." I look at Ted. "If you are guilty of adultery, apologize to Claire."

"Wait a minute—it does matter to me!" Claire explodes.

I stand up to confront her. "All that matters is you have each other. Trust me, lose a spouse—whether from divorce or death—and you might never recover. I'd give *anything* to have Arthur back."

Claire and Ted glare at each other.

"Did you have an affair?" she asks him.

"No, Claire, I did not."

"There!" I exclaim. "Now, can we just sit together and enjoy this beautiful early summer evening? I have much I need to tell you both."

Ted reaches for Claire's hand and holds it tightly.

"Claire, I'm sorry I did not explain to you why the lipstick was on my shirt. Hear me out. Shirley Patterson hired me last month to audit her finances. She's a young, upcoming country-western music star."

He locks eyes with me. "I expect neither of you have heard of Shirley yet, but you will. She's a fantastic artist. I took her to supper, and like I said, sometimes these newcomers don't know when to stop drinking. Afterall, I'm footing the bill." His eyes are on his wife again.

Claire is trembling. I see how much she loves Ted.

He takes her hand. "After dinner, I walked Shirley to her apartment door. She was three sheets to the wind when she hugged me goodbye and stumbled against my shirt." Emotion threads his voice.

I feel life is improving.

"That's how I got the lipstick on my shirt, honey."

Honey, not Claire. We're making progress.

They come together like a magnet draws them. Claire rises on her tiptoes and kisses Ted. It's not a peck, trust me.

I'd give a lot for someone like Tom to kiss me like that. I am proud of myself. My marriage-counselor skills worked quite well tonight.

26

Monday, May 15

YESTERDAY, CLAIRE DROVE me to Columbia in her Buick and let me out at the First United Methodist Church. I had missed enough Sunday School and church services to accumulate some guilt. I owed gratitude to God for His guidance and deliverance from evil.

Besides, I wanted to give the rekindled lovebirds a chance to peck at each other. I don't think Ted will make the same mistake again. Telling the truth is important. Virtue avoids bad consequences in a marriage. I truly believe my family has love embedded in their souls.

But I did not spend the night with Lorene; rather, invited myself to Ellie Simpson's B & B. The house feels like home, simply because it was once mine. With Ellie's parents away on a camping trip, she is delighted to have my company. And she's read about Ted's accident.

We are seated at the kitchen bar drinking our morning coffee.

"Is there a lawsuit against Ted since the driver of the other vehicle died?" Ellie poses an idea that never crossed my mind.

"No one has said anything about a lawsuit."

"Maybe Ted and Claire don't want to worry you," Ellie says.

I wonder now why I came here for solace; it's not working. She's a quick-study and realizes her suggestion has upset me.

"So . . .how was the church service yesterday?" Ellie inquires.

I am relieved to move on with a less-worrisome conversation.

"Brother Kenny always gives it straight to us," I reply.

Ellie tilts her head. "I don't know much about church. My parents never took me. They lean to the liberal side of thought."

"Really?" I am taken back by her comment. "I would have never thought that. They seem like such good parents."

"People can be good without being Christians," Ellie sets me straight. "I'm sorry, that did not come out right."

"No, it did. But you should also know that the Bible says our goodness will not earn us a spot in Heaven. We must be born again into God's Kingdom." I realize Ellie will not understand any of that.

She glares at me.

"I know, I'll give you a New Testament to read, then we will talk about faith and goodness," I decide. "I need to get dressed now."

"But you didn't have breakfast!" she protests.

"I have too much on my mind to be hungry." I stand up. "Do you mind driving me to a rental dealership in Columbia?"

"Sure, I need to shop for groceries. It will be my pleasure."

Thirty minutes later we are ready to leave. The drive into town is pleasant, the day promising to be clear with temps in the eighties.

Ellie lets me off at Foster's Rental Services. I know the owner. Bill Foster was one of my students when I taught high school eons ago. We were both a lot younger then. He inherited his father's dealership and has done quite well. So, I ask at the counter to speak with him.

"He's busy in the office, can I help you?" the saleslady says.

"You could, but I prefer talking to Bill." I am set in my ways.

"Okay . . ." she rolls her coffee-brown eyes and points to a vacant chair in one corner. "You can wait over there. It might be a while."

"I have the time."

But one hour is ridiculous. Bill comes through the door behind the counter and speaks with Gladys Saleslady, then she points at me.

His eyes alight. "Mrs. Powell!"

I can hear his salutation all the way across the large display room. I stand up and wait for his arrival. He's gained fifty pounds since high school. And obviously wears a toupee. But his smile is the same.

"What can we do for you today?" Bill inquires.

"My car was stolen on Friday and the guy wrecked it."

"Oh, I'm sorry to hear that."

"Feel sorry for the guy; he died in the crash," I reply. "I was thinking of buying a more practical car, but have decided I'd rather lease one. Do you have that kind of service?" I look at him good.

"I'm afraid we are only temporary rentals, Mrs. Powell," he tells me with a grin. I always liked Bill; he was so pleasant as a youngster.

"But I will send you over to Thatcher," he qualifies. "He's a good friend and will treat you right. He works for the Audi Dealership."

A foreign car? I think to myself, unsure if I want my money spent out of the USA. I am a patriot, down to my tippytoes.

"How did you get here?" Bill inquires as he hands me his business card with Thatcher's cell number scribbled on the back.

"Ellie Simpson drove me," I reply.

"Read about her loss last year. Butch was a cornerstone in Columbia and we all miss him. Got a rough start as a teen, but came out okay." He looks at me for a comment. Butch is Detective Lloyd Peters, shot and burned in his apartment last Thanksgiving.

"Ellie's a trooper," I add, end of discussion.

This need-to-know thing prohibits me from sharing details about Detective Chico's belief that the Mafia killed Butch as payback.

"I suppose I'll need a ride to the dealership."

"No problem, Gladys will take you over."

"Thank you, Bill. I'm proud you've done so well."

"A high complement coming from you, Mrs. Powell. I never could pull more than a B grade in your Biology Class." He chuckles.

* * *

I drove out of the Audi Dealership in a midnight-blue Audi A4 hybrid sedan that has been driven only two-thousand miles. Thatcher said I could purchase the car after six months, using the money I paid for monthly rental as a down payment. I am not interested at this time.

I feel safer in a different vehicle, hoping the Mafia thugs will not easily recognize the Audi as mine. I'm tired of people trying to kill me.

The drive north of Columbia is familiar. I try not to think of all the times Arthur and I took this trek on our way home.

Lorene does not respond to the doorbell and I wonder if she's home. I'll investigate. I find my friend seated on the back porch.

"Dorothy!" She shuffles to her feet.

She says it with such gusto I think of Dorothy in the Wizard of Oz film when she finally found her way home after a tornado.

"I want you to see my new car—well, my rental," I tell her.

She opens the screen door for me.

"Let's go inside the house first and I'll fix us a glass of lemonade."

"Sounds like a plan." I trail her.

"Then, my friend, you can tell me all about what's happened since we were last together on Friday." Lorene refers to dropping me off at the Police Station after my BMW was stolen on court square.

"Well, maybe not everything," I comment.

We carry our glasses of lemonade out on the back porch where we sit in the hanging swing. I am thirsty and drink like a sailor.

"What were those packets of coffee on the bar for?" I inquire.

"That's not a popular subject in my house," Lorene pipes.

"Why not?" *It's just coffee*, I think to myself.

"Cyn orders the coffee from a European Company in London," she replies. "I don't get what's wrong with Folgers or Columbian."

I don't think comparing brands of coffee is worth my effort, so I don't comment. Gently rocking in the swing has a calming effect.

"I assume your BMW is in the repair shop and that is why you are driving a rental car," Lorene utters between sips of coffee.

I can tell she likes Cyn's brand, but will never admit it.

"You assume wrong, Lorene. The thief totaled my car and died in the process," I explain. "Somebody cut the brake line."

"What?" Lorene nearly falls out of the swing.

I cannot help but smile. "I know, the bad guys missed again. I was supposed to be driving my car, not the thief."

Lorene shakes her head. "You truly do have nine lives. God must send his angels every day to watch over you, Dorothy."

I smile at the image of my guardian angel floating over me.

"A nice thought, Lorene but none of us will escape Death."

"Don't say that, Dorothy!" Lorene is distressed and wrings her hands. "I don't want to think of losing anyone else I love."

I touch her hand. "That's so sweet. I'm not going anywhere yet."

"Promise?"

I spend the morning helping Lorene clean out closets upstairs to make room for more of Graham and Cynthia's clothes. She shows me a picture of the house they plan on building next spring. I don't know if the newlyweds will share in utility costs and other home purchases.

"I know you said you'd share your bed, but I need to return to Claire's. I still have not told her about the attempts on my life."

"Maybe you shouldn't worry her."

"Avoid the truth? No." I am adamant. "I witnessed for myself how avoidance can harm a relationship. Claire and Ted had a huge misunderstanding the other night, and I need to see for myself how they are doing." They might need a little more counseling.

"What is Claire's problem?" Lorene asks.

I look at her and think of what Captain Colbert told me.

"Sorry, Lorene. It's a need-to-know thing, and I don't think Claire will appreciate me sharing details even with my best friend," I explain.

"Oh, pooh! I love a good story."

Before I spill my guts, I pick up my purse to leave.

"Wait, Dorothy! Please don't go!" Lorene calls after me.

"But I promised myself I'd see after Claire tonight."

27

Friday, May 19

I BROKE MY PROMISE to myself and stayed with Lorene all week. I did not want to miss our regular Canasta card game Friday afternoon at the Senior Citizen Center. Seeing few people welcomed me, I may have made an error in judgment in coming. But Lorene is on my side.

"Don't let those busybodies bother you, Dorothy," she tells me as we walk across the hall to line up for lunch. "They're just jealous."

"Of me?" I whisper, leaning close to Lorene's ear. "Why? Do they have a death wish?" I straighten up and try to look composed. I'm not at all. I feel all their stares—from people I used to consider my friends. I see them whispering, gossiping, about me.

"Let's get some lunch and eat in peace, okay?" she suggests.

I sigh. What other choice do I have? I'm already here.

Lunch consists of fried chicken, smashed white potatoes, green beans from a can, and peach cobbler. Rolls are optional. I had one.

"What do you want to drink?" Lorene stands in front of the counter holding carafes of sweet and unsweet tea. Coffee is an option.

"Water," I decide and fill my plastic glass with ice cubes then add water from a dispenser. I am bent on losing more weight. Since this past Christmas, I have lost thirty pounds. But I am tall and carry my weight well. I wear a size ten pants now, and a size twelve blouse.

Lorene fills her glass with sweet tea and we take our food to a table. Two people I've never seen before finish their meals and leave.

"Do you know those people?" I ask Lorene.

"The Carters. They moved here two weeks ago from California."

"I can't keep up with progress in Columbia. I don't fit anywhere."

Lorene licks peach cobbler off her spoon. "That's not true, Dorothy. You will always be a crowning citizen of this county."

"I'm reconsidering Detective Chico's and Captain Colbert's offer to put me in Protective Custody. I don't feel safe on the streets anymore." I consider telling Lorene about the young man stalking me.

Maybe I'm paranoid. But every day or so, the same face shows up. Across a street from me. Or at the gas station while I pump. I've even seen him at the grocery store where Claire shops. Then maybe it's only a coincidence that we do the same things on the same days.

"How long would you need to be gone with a new identity?" Lorene asks as she polishes off her dessert with sips of tea.

"Could be awhile," I reply. "Maybe a year or two—until the people who have been trying to kill me are captured and behind bars."

"Lordy Mercy, Dorothy! Don't leave me."

I chuckle. "Are you going to protect me?"

"We can have food delivered to my house and never go out."

I smile at her foolishness. "Folks will talk."

She tries to decide what I mean.

"What about Canasta on Fridays?" Lorene asks me.

"Well . . . I would definitely miss that."

"See. You cannot possibly leave the life you love."

"I'm done eating." I see that she is too. And weary of thought. Let's get out of here. I don't feel the same warmth I used to."

"What about our card game?"

"Text Lizzy and Jane and tell them we're moving the game to your house," I decide. "Do it now, and let's go." I grab my purse.

Like an obedient daughter, Lorene sends the message.

We're in my rental car whizzing down the highway when Lorene receives responses. "They're coming. I told them around two."

"Good, I need to share something with you first."

"What? Is it bad?" Her eyes squint with intrigue.

I laugh. "I think you like *bad*, friend. It spices up your life."

"If it's something you must share, tell me now."

Lorene loves a good story so I inhale deeply, my hands tight on the steering wheel, and begin the drama. "Well, there's this strange man—he keeps popping up everywhere I go." I glance over at her.

"No . . ." Lorene looks around as if the stalker might pop up in my backseat. Her gaze settles on me. "What does he look like?"

"Young. Casually dressed—no obvious tattoos. I spotted him at the dry cleaner's when I picked up my Easter suit last week. He was at the bookstore in Nashville when I was with Claire."

I look at Lorene. "He's even driven past Claire's house."

"You recognized his car?"

"Yes. Same license plate," I answer.

"Shouldn't you tell Detective Chico about your stalker?"

I lift my shoulders slightly. A shrug. "Could be a coincidence."

"And maybe he works for the Russian Mafia."

"Maybe he was hired to protect me."

"That's a naïve answer, Dorothy," Lorene cautions me. "Did you ever consider that this man may have murdered Zoey Jackson?"

"No, I haven't gotten that far," I reply, now more concerned.

I turn off the highway into Lorene's long gravel driveway that takes us to the top of the hill where her lovely home looms.

"Please report him to Chico," Lorene insists as she exits the passenger side of the Audi. "She can run his license plate number."

"Okay, but not today. Let's play cards with our friends."

Lorene opens the door and we go inside. She makes an old-fashioned pot of Folgers coffee and we sit at the bar to drink it.

Lizzy and Jane arrive on time and the game begins.

Jane is my partner and I draw for the first deal. I measure exactly one-half the deck, hoping for a perfect deal of thirteen cards each. Jane places one card sideways in the caddy to separate the last eight cards from the rest of the deck. I deal perfectly and earn our team 100 points.

But Canasta is not the only game we are playing.

"Where is your red BMW, Dorothy?" Lizzy asks.

Lorene pipes, "I told you it was stolen last week."

"I heard the thief ran it into a ditch and was killed," Jane reports. "The newspaper article gave sketchy details of the explosion."

I look at my fantastic card hand, certain that the police had not divulged to the newspaper that my car brakes had been cut. And I won't tell this need-to-know detail even to my card buddies.

28

Saturday, May 20

I WAKE UP IN CLAIRE'S guest bedroom Saturday morning. My ears tune to the sounds in the house. Birds twitter and tweet outside the window as I climb out of bed and stretch my stiff body.

I had left the house earlier this week without telling my darlings about the times I've nearly "bit the dust." That's an ol' cowboy saying, but it seems fit for a cowgirl like me that never rides off in the sunset with the handsome hero. Thomas Kessler certainly ran out on me.

Everyone bites the dust at one time or another, I realize. Some are young and plain unlucky. Some are middle-aged and die of diseases. Then, there is me. Soon to be turning eighty-three. I am no old fool.

Simply because I do realize my time is running out on earth to accomplish whatever it is God means for me to do. If only a voice in my head would tell me how to keep away from trouble.

I take a quick shower and dress for the new day. After a quick prayer, and vowing to myself to find a place of my own today, I venture into the kitchen. The two lovebirds have had a good week, I can tell.

They are cuddled together at the bar, whispering nothings—at least nothing they are sharing with me. I clear my throat.

"Mama!" Claire spins around on the barstool. "I did not hear you come in last night. How late was it?"

"After eleven," I reply as I meander around the counter in search of a cup of morning coffee. "Lorene begged me to spend the night, but her son Graham and his new wife have moved in with her."

"I know she has upstairs bedrooms," Claire offers a solution.

"The kids have the run of the upstairs." I gaze at my daughter. "Besides, I flip and turn over too many times while trying to sleep to share a bed with Lorene. So around ten, I decided to come home."

Ted smiles. "I like the sound of that, Mama. Home."

Every time Ted calls me Mama, it stirs my heart. Before Arthur died, he called me Dorothy. That felt so cold and I am a warm person.

He is dressed in a pinstripe suit with a white shirt and sunflower-yellow tie. He appears healthy; less sugar intake I suspect. He pecks Claire on the cheek and she holds him tight, like he might get away.

"Enjoy Mama, honey. The office needs me for a few hours."

"We still have a dinner date tonight?" Claire smiles at him like the Cheshire Cat in the *Alice and Wonderland* story. She's smitten.

I hear a horn honking in the driveway.

"That's Kenneth, I need to go, honey." He tries to pull away.

Nothing doing. One more kiss for the road, he gives Claire.

I am basking in glory. I feel like a successful marriage counselor since I was the person that clarified their near-fatal misunderstanding. Their argument over lipstick on his shirt might have turned into an explosion that blew up any hope of salvaging their relationship.

All is well that seems well, I accept my conclusion.

When Ted has left, I sit at the bar drinking coffee with Claire.

"Did you have a good week in Columbia, Mama?"

"Fair to middling," I reply. That's a farming term I'd heard Arthur say many times over the years. It means average in judging cattle.

"Okay, what kind of trouble have you stirred up this time?"

"How much time do you have, Claire?"

* * *

The real estate sales lady picks me up at one p.m. It had taken me more than an hour to describe to Claire my several encounters with danger. She could not believe I had kept all of that from her. I explained it was because I loved her and didn't want her to worry about me. But she cried, anyhow. I did not tell her about the young man stalking me, unsure if it were true or just my overworked imagination.

Tanya is a broker for a new real estate company in Nashville. The last two years have been prosperous for her since residents from states that taxed personal income have moved in droves to Tennessee.

As a result, there is a shortage of properties—both rentals and houses on the market for sale. Thus, Nashville has grown by leaps and bounds with skyscrapers leaping up like mushrooms overnight.

"The market is hot," Tanya explains. Rents have nearly doubled since Covid 19 struck in 2020. What you see today may be gone tomorrow." I know this is a sales pitch to get a quick commitment.

Still, I want to view for myself what Brentwood and the Cool Springs market offers for rent. We drive past apartment complexes and condo developments for hours. I remain undecided about what to do.

Perhaps I don't want to pay the price of high rents. Or, deep down, I don't want to tie myself down to a property. And why is that? Do I expect Tom to show up? Do I want to travel around the world?

I did two years ago after I threw Arthur to the wind.

If I travel, I could disappear into a foreign country where the Russian Mafia cannot find me. I'd change my name and become someone else. I would not need the help of a Protection Agency.

I should check the costs of travel abroad and forget renting.

"Well, Mrs. Powell, what are you thinking?" Tanya asks.

"Honestly, you've shown me enough properties. They are all nice but very expensive. Don't get me wrong, I can afford the rent. I just don't believe I want to be tied down at this stage of my life."

The light in Tanya's gaze dims. She is disappointed and I feel guilty for taking advantage of her. Time spent with me has resulted in loss of income for her. But I am not yet ready to settle down in Nashville.

Buying would lock me into a commitment for life at my age.

"I apologize, Tanya." I remove a $100 bill from my purse and hand it to her before I exit her Mazda at Claire's house.

"Really, I should not accept this," Tanya says.

But I can see relief in her expression.

"Please do not deny me this pleasure. Giving blesses me. I've had a pleasant afternoon and learned a great deal about the rental market. I promise if I decide to rent or buy, you will be the first person I call. Okay?" I place the money in her palm. "Please, for me."

"You are very generous, Mrs. Powell. Thank you."

"No, thank you. And have a great rest of the day."

Claire opens the front door for me. "Did you find something?"

"I found a lot, but I'm not renting." I enter the foyer.

"Why not?"

I shrug. "I'm not ready, Claire. I want to travel."

"Alone?"

"If I have to—you once said you'd take a trip with me."

"What about all the murders involving you?" Claire reminds me. "Will Detective Chico allow you to leave the country?"

Now, that is something I have not considered. I do not think I am a suspect in Gloria Bolton's death, but life can flip on a dime.

"What do you want to do, Mama?"

"For a little while longer, I'll hang out with friends in Columbia. After my facelift in early June, I'll stay with you to recover. When I feel comfortable going out in public, I'll make travel plans."

I am so proud of myself for finally making a decision.

Claire smiles and places a fond hand on my shoulder.

"Mama, you know you are always welcome to stay with us for as long as you want. Ted and I only want what is best for you. Besides, the kids want to throw a big birthday party for you in June."

"That is very sweet, we'll see."

"No, we won't see. There will be a party and you will be there. I insist," Claire says. "Mama, you deserve it! We all love you."

Her words roll over me like warm ocean water. Feeling loved is a wonderful gift. Not everyone has a fantastic family like mine.

29

Thursday, May 25

IT IS THE FOURTH THURSDAY of the month and I intend to keep my hair appointment with Gloria my hairdresser for over a decade. I trust her to always do a good job and that's important. Today, I need a trim and color before Dr. Sharra tears up my face and gives it a redo.

I exit my rental Audi in front of the clapboard house that is nestled in the foothills of Maury County. Gloria's Hair Salon is stationed in an addition tagged onto the back of her house. I don't knock since I am expected at ten a.m. I know my way through the maze of compact rooms. Odors of hair color chemicals and shampoo sting my nostrils as I enter the salon proper. Gloria is teasing a customer's golden hair.

"Oh, hi, Mrs. Powell. I wondered if you'd come?"

"Why wouldn't I, Gloria?"

The hairdresser only shrugs as I notice she has a new customer I do not recognize. "Elizabeth Wright," the stranger introduces herself.

"Dorothy Powell," I return the salutation, rudely staring.

"No, we haven't met, Dorothy. My husband and I just moved to Columbia two weeks ago. I saw Gloria's ad in the newspaper."

I turn to Gloria, surprised. "You advertise for customers?"

"I guess you haven't heard. Mrs. Crabtree and Janie Copeland recently passed from Covid—could be a new strain of the virus."

"No, I wasn't aware." I place my purse in a vacant chair. "I've been between my daughter's house in Brentwood and Columbia since I sold my house late February. How is your family doing, Gloria?"

She lifts one shoulder, her hands deep into Elizabeth's dyed golden hair to set her hairdo. "Got a granddaughter with the virus, but she'll be fine. Fatigue seems to be the worst of her side effects."

"I'm afraid this monster virus will come back to haunt us in a different uniform every year. Winters seem the worst," I prophesy.

"You got that right!" someone calls out from the doorway.

"Gerry?" I know that voice and turn around.

Gloria Bolton's widower stands there.

"I know . . . my barber has the virus so I called Gloria. I wanted to avoid crowds at all costs. How have you been, Dorothy?"

"I can't say enough how sorry I am you lost your wife," my hairdresser tells him. "It seems a lot of people are grieving these days."

"Life dumps us the unexpected." He gazes at me.

My heart goes out to this man, someone who would never hurt a fly. His wife's death is partially my fault, though unintentional. I feel it's pertinent I say something. "We're all sorry Gloria died."

Seeing his expression gives me pause.

"My wife didn't just die, Dorothy, she was murdered."

I am so embarrassed. He knows I exchanged lattes with Gloria but the others in the room do not. I should be the one rotting in a grave. Yet, I live to suffer for my sins. He throws a hand.

"I know, saying I'm sorry won't change anything."

"Oh, Dorothy, it's not your fault she died," he walks toward me. "I don't hold grudges. Cancel my appointment, Gloria."

"Are you sure? I'll get Dorothy started then get to you."

"Yeah, you're busy, so I'll come back tomorrow."

Gerry leaves through the outside door to the garden.

"What was that about?" Elizabeth Wright inquires.

"A murder mystery that has stumped us all," I reply.

"Twenty dollars, Mrs. Wright. Shall I book you for next month?"

"Yes, please. Dorothy, good to meet you."

"Goes two ways."

It's my turn. Gloria sets out her chemicals to color my hair. When she is finished, strands of my gray hair will be tinted a light blond. The process is called "low lights" as in opposition to "high lights" that younger people get. The process takes up to an hour to complete.

I tip Gloria an extra $5 when I pay my tab.

"Will you be here next month?" Gloria inquires.

"I'll call and cancel if I can't."

My next stop is with my primary care physician.

Dr. Sharra wanted me to have a physical and blood tests to make sure I am healthy enough to be put to sleep for the cosmetic surgery he'll perform. I was due for a six-month checkup in late June, anyhow.

Dr. Robert Hammons has been practicing medicine for thirty years in Columbia. I want to get in and out of that office as fast as I can, and I'm not in the mood to be practiced on.

His secretary Julie sits at the front desk, pampering her face with a powder puff as she looks in a mirror. Then she sees me.

"Oh. I didn't notice you coming in, Mrs. Powell."

"I'm here for my six-month checkup—a little early," I tell her.

"I'll let Dr. Hammons know you are here." She grabs a landline.

I take a seat and peruse a *Better Homes & Garden* magazine. Mostly advertisement, but a few interesting recipes for dieters.

Ten minutes pass. My name is called from the doorway.

The compact examining room is equipped with a small desk in one corner that hosts a variety of useful tools in the medical profession.

I wait to be seen, not so patiently. What if I have something wrong with me? People my age always get something dreadful. Arthur was healthy, yet he died anyway—at the hand of an assassin. I wonder how I will die. I don't expect it to be pretty. I start to drift off to sleep.

"Ah . . . my favorite patient!" Dr. Hammons hails from the doorway. "How are you feeling today, Dorothy?" He approaches.

I like that Robert's hair is a thick salt-and-pepper and he's gym-toned at sixty-five-years old. His face has a few battle scars from aging, but his personality makes up for any disadvantages. He's recently divorced, and I wonder who he is dating. Someone younger, I bet.

"Feeling fine for an old codger like me," I respond to his question.

"We all age, Mrs. Powell. Don't beat yourself up over a few added wrinkles since we last met." I'll give him a C for bedside manner.

I rub my cheek with a hand. *Do I have more wrinkles?*

"The reason I'm here a month early is because I'm scheduled to have a cosmetic-surgery procedure in early June." I inform him I need my blood test results faxed to Dr. Lyle Sharra's office.

"No problem. Hop up on the examining table," he orders as he sits on a barstool and runs it across the linoleum floor.

"How is your vision?" His mouth smells like peppermint.

"Fine, I don't need glasses."

"That's marvelous." He flicks a stick in my mouth to pry it open to see down my throat. "Good there, too." He rolls back in his chair. "Did you fast before you had blood drawn this morning?"

I blink. "I thought you'd take my blood while I am here."

"No, we require you not eat anything after midnight on the day the blood is drawn," he reminds me. "Did you forget?"

I stiffen. Does he think I have dementia?

"I suppose I did. Can I do it tomorrow morning?"

"Sure. We'll take care of everything else today," he decides.

"Thank you."

He makes some notes on my chart.

"What time does your lab open tomorrow?"

"Seven a.m.," he replies. "Go straight to the lab. My nurse will give you a form to take with you before you leave the office today."

I am finished forty-five minutes later.

As I sit in the Audi, just like Claire taught me, I key a reminder in my cell phone to wake up early tomorrow morning for my blood test. And a second reminder to start my fast tonight at midnight.

Then I phone Lorene to see if I can spend the night.

"As long as you don't sock me in your sleep," she teases.

I drive to Walmart and go inside to purchase food for our supper. The place is a zoo with every describable type of animal perusing the nearly-empty grocery shelves for food items. I walk to the back of the store where the bakery sells fresh meats, salads, fried foods, and pizzas.

Unsure if Graham and Cynthia will join us for supper, I select the large deluxe pizza with everything on it but Grandma. It appears large enough to easily feed four. Then I cash out at the self-help register.

Out of the corner of my eye, I spot *that* man again. The one I've seen too often to be a coincidence. He fiddles with his phone.

Is he texting about me? Does he work for the Mafia?

I am going to find out. With my pizza snug in a large plastic bag, I chase him out of the store through the automatic double doors.

"Wait up, mister!" I call out, nearly tripping on my own feet.

He does not appear to hear me. Or he's avoiding me.

I pick up speed and almost trip again. God help me, old age is a hindrance! "Wait up, young man, I need to talk to you. Please!"

I watch as he scrambles into a truck and backs out of the parking space. He drives in the opposite direction. And I am pissed off!

Who is my stalker?

* * *

Officer Joseph Hale is on the phone with Detective Chico as he exits the Walmart parking lot in his black SUV.

"Dorothy Powell made me," he reports. "She even tried to chase me down. What do you want me to do?" Joe waits for instructions.

"Stop following her. I'll send someone else to tail her."

"Sorry." He ends the call, feeling defeated by an old woman.

30

LORENE AND I WATCH a movie on the Hallmark Channel after supper. I burp pizza a few times then recall I have to fast after midnight. "I'd better drink a large glass of water." I go to the kitchen.

"Hurry up, you're missing the best part!" Lorene hails from her recliner. "The guy gets the girl. Wow! I wish I could get kissed like that." She giggles like a teenager. I think she should date again.

The movie ends around 9:20 and Lorene shuts off the TV.

"You never said how your doctor's appointment went."

"I appear healthy according to Dr. Hammons, but I have to fast after midnight and return to the clinic early tomorrow morning to have my blood drawn. The lab will email the results to Dr. Sharra as requested. I don't think I'll have a problem with the procedure."

Lorene erects the recliner. With feet firmly planted on the carpet, she leans forward and says, "Other than your face will look like someone has beaten you up. Healing will take weeks."

I frown. "Don't remind me."

"I read where facial wounds are painful."

"Dr. Google." I chuckle. "Soon we won't need a human doctor."

"You trust a computer?" Lorene stands, stretches, and yawns.

"Google seems to have an answer for everything."

"Well, tell it goodnight. Because I am going to bed."

"I think I'll stretch out on the sofa and read for a while."

"Are you going to sleep there all night?" Lorene glares.

"I might. I squirm a lot in bed lately and I don't want to disturb your rest, Lorene." I grab the Afghan. "Go to bed. I'll be fine."

"Well, if you change your mind, you know your way to my bedroom." Lorene looms over me like she is my mentor.

"Any other motherly advice?" I look up at her as I lay on the sofa.

"If you can't fall sleep, warm up some milk, or have one of those chocolate kisses in the jar on the breakfast bar," Lorene suggests.

"Dr. Google again?"

She nods. "I'm just trying to be a good hostess."

"Goodnight, Lorene, I am fine. I'm just not sleepy."

"Okay." She turns away.

I hear the pattering of bare feet crossing the wood floor and a door closing at the other side of the den. A nightlight is on in the kitchen to guide my way if I need to potty during the night. I remove my novel from my big purse and open it to page 209. This author likes to describe naughty love scenes. While I'm reading, I picture myself in the arms of Thomas Kessler, a man I will probably never see again.

Oh, Arthur! Please forgive me for my infidelity.

31

Friday, May 26

LIGHT FILTERS THROUGH THE bedroom blinds and wakes me. I get up and tiptoe into the master bathroom to pee while Lorene snores in a death grip. I gave up the sofa at 2 a.m. this morning and crawled in bed with Lorene. My phone registers 6:30 a.m. The clinic lab opens at seven, so I'm not at all too early to leave and get the job done.

The sun is a red ball of fire on the eastern horizon as I drive over rolling wooded hills into the city of Columbia. The air is cool so I have the windows down in my rented Audi. I inhale and exhale. *Life.*

A few vehicles are already parked in the clinic lot. I park as close to the front door as I can, lock the car, and approach the premises.

A sign on the door states, "Masks required."

Covid has pumped up again. It's not supposed to do that in warm weather. I wonder what variation has broken out in the world and moved to America. The virus is not welcome, but I am forced to adapt.

I pilfer through my purse for a mask. I don't have one. It wasn't required yesterday for treatment, but apparently it is today.

I check in at the front desk with the male secretary. "Dorothy Jean Powell. 6/25/1939," I give him my name and birthdate then wave the form I received yesterday from the nurse to visit the lab this morning.

He hands me a mask. "Go on back to the lab, Ms. Powell."

No need to respond, I go through a door and find the room off the hallway where a nurse sits at a computer and takes my form.

"It will be a few minutes. You can sit over there."

No need to comment, I sit down to wait with another woman. She's on her phone—no surprise there. The device has become our lifeline of communication to the World Wide Web. Our great and grands would not know how to survive without the device.

I'm sad at the thought and close my eyes and offer up a prayer to God. *Thank you for this day. I pray I am not making a mistake in having surgery at my age. Please tell me. Give me signal. Or a sign will do.*

I pause to reflect on my life. *Amen.*

"Dorothy Powell."

"Yes." I open my eyes and see a technician standing over me.

"Come with me."

I obey and moments later a needle is in the curve of my arm and red blood pours out into a glass vial. I relax my gripped fist to allow the red liquid to flow more freely. The technician takes five vials.

"Are you on blood thinners, Mrs. Powell?"

"No."

"Wear this band-aid for ten minutes and you should be fine."

"Thank you," I tell the technician. Joanna is her name.

"You are most welcome. Have a grand day." She hands me my paperwork. "Take this form back to the front desk. You are done."

32

Sunday, June 25

A MONTH HAS PASSED and life has gone on as usual. Except today is my birthday. I have been staying with Claire since the day of my surgery, trying to avoid Columbia and any dreadful hitman looking for me. I am up early this morning for breakfast. Claire has gone to church.

So far, I haven't seen Ted today. I am once again "alone."

After showering and dressing, I spend the morning reading a spineless novel with no particular appeal. Just biding time until my party starts at two this afternoon. It is a gift to have my extended family around me on my special day—which makes me wonder what presents I will receive at my party. Although turning eighty-three does not thrill me since I've moved another notch toward my demise, I am reminded that Christians should not fear death. We are to trust that Jesus will greet us at Heaven's Door, then lead the way into Eternal Bliss.

Except I have no idea what forever will look like. But the Bible clearly states that people will no longer be sad or cry or hurt.

What's wrong with that?

Lunch is a ham sandwich with salty chips. Ted is home, but in his office with the door shut. Who am I to ask questions?

My family arrives shortly before two. It is a fantastic day outdoors, sprinkled with sunlight that highlight the rich shades of green foliage.

I am blessed to have my loved ones around me.

"Blow out your candles and make a wish, GG!"

The request comes from my great-granddaughter June. No hard task since there are eight large and three smaller candles perched on the top of a vanilla-cream cake Claire ordered from an exclusive pastry shop. No doubt the contents will be exceptional and calorie-loaded.

I look at my family one by one. "This is too much, loves."

June's older brother Billy does not agree, and runs over to give me help blowing out the candles. I halt him with my hand.

"My job, Billy." I take in a huge breath.

Everyone laughs at my statement then comments on how well I look today. Most do not know I had my face lifted in early June.

I inhale deeply but delay the moment to blow out the candles on my birthday cake. Then I wonder if this will be my last time. One can't be too careful fulfilling the task. I make a wish—private and foolish probably—and take in a huge breath. *Here goes . . .*

I blow hard and extinguish the candles. They go up in smoke and hover momentarily over the cake. It makes me think of souls in flight to Heaven. People burn brightly until they don't. I look at my family and pray Arthur is happy in Heaven. Even if he doesn't enjoy music.

"Presents! Presents!" June hops around the table loaded with wrapped gifts. All for me, I presume. Far too much fanfare in my estimation. But if a party makes my family feel better, so be it.

One by one I open my treasures. Benjamin, Claire's son, gives me a $50 gift card to Macy's. I usually shop at Burkes for their reduced merchandise, but I know Ben wants to reward me for a long life.

Ted and Claire's gift is a snuggly green robe with matching slippers for next winter's cold spell. I thank them with a hug. Helen and Patrick present me with a new iPhone. I tense at the idea of learning new tricks at my age. Technology is a puzzle and a challenge for me.

"Open mine, GG!" June screams.

Her mother Helen cautions her to be quiet. She isn't. I love that no one can squelch the enthusiasm of children for parties. When they are older, they will look back and cherish their innocent antics. Life will only get more difficult and challenging for them. They will encounter people who are unkind and deceitful. I feel sorry for them.

What am I thinking? This is a party not a wake.

"What's this?" Claire picks up the last package. "Who is this from?" she asks everyone. All shake their heads. I blink back tears.

If that is from you Thomas, I swear I am going to kill you.

"What is it, Mama? Are you sick?" Ted notes my despair.

"Will, uh, you excuse me?" I grab the gift and retreat down the hallway to the guest bedroom. My heart is beating triple time. I am an old fool in love with an idea. I want to shred this package and never open it. Yet, it sits on the bed staring back at me. I can't do this.

I sit in a chair beside the dresser and pray to God I am not going to stoke out. I'm sick to my stomach that I feel compelled to open that gift. I cannot do this. I despise Thomas. I hate that I love him.

A knock comes at the door.

I do not answer it.

"Mama, it's Claire. Are you alright?"

I do not answer her.

"Mama, let me in this room!" she calls out louder.

I will not answer her.

"Mama, it's Ted. Did we upset you with the party?"

My silence gives him my answer.

"Dorothy! Open this door right now or I will knock it down!"

I wake up as if from a dream. "No, don't, I'm coming."

I crack the door and stare out at Ted and Claire.

"I'm fine." I hold on to the knob prepared to slam the door.

"You're not fine, Mama." Claire pushes the door open and steps inside. "I have this, Ted. Let me talk to Mama alone."

She closes the door in Ted's face and leans against it.

"Is it that package? Does it upset you?"

I nod.

"You think it's a bomb?"

I shake my head no.

"You think it's from *him*."

I nod affirmatively.

"Throw it away then. Ignore it."

"I can't," I utter.

"Okay then, we'll open it together."

I nod, terrified.

She shakes the package as if it might contain something sinister. The idea makes me smile for the first time since I laid eyes on it.

Claire rips off the brown paper and holds up my gift.

"It's a book! A children's book!" she exclaims.

Double D-D! I silently curse. Thomas Kessler, jerk, you just put a target on my back. If the Russian Mafia finds out I have this hot item, they will tear Claire's house apart to get to me. I am mortified.

Later, when everyone has gone home but Claire and Ted, they ask me too many questions about the book that I cannot answer. Or won't. This is a problem I will have to take care of on my own. I do not want to involve my family in matters that might get them killed.

"It's a joke, loves," I blow off their remarks.

Claire is unconvinced. Theodore doesn't seem to care; he has other things on his mind. I hope not a woman that interests him.

I go to bed that night with so many questions plaguing my mind, I have difficulty sleeping. But one thing I know: God is on my side.

33

Monday, June 26

THE DAY AFTER I celebrated my eighty-third birthday, on Monday, I drove my midnight-blue Audi A4 hybrid car to Columbia. Thatcher had treated me right and sold me the rental car for $30 grand. I was pleased the car had less than 3,000 miles registered on the odometer.

I was at Detective Chico's office by nine a.m. but she wasn't there.

"When will she be back?" I queried her secretary.

"She took the day off," Blake replied.

"How can detectives do that when there are murders to be solved?" I glare down at him. "Sorry, I'm in a bad mood."

"You can leave a written message if you like," he says.

"No, will you call over to Captain Colbert's office and see if she's in today?" I ask nicely. He stares up at me. "What?"

"Don't you know how to use a phone?" I testily ask.

"Yes. I do not see the point."

I sassily park a hand on one hip. "Call her office," I insist.

"Right now, I'm in the middle of typing a report, Mrs. Powell." He scribbles a phone number on a yellow sticky and hands it to me.

"Thank you." *What happened to male chivalry?*

I step out into the hall for privacy then manage to open my Apple phone and not eat it, just like Helen taught me. After punching in a series of numbers, I finally reach Captain Colbert's office.

"How may I direct you?" queries a female voice.

"Are you a computer or a real person?" I ask.

"Real. Are you?"

"Cute," I reply. "May I speak with Captain Colbert."

"Is this a scheduled call?"

"No, it's spontaneous and important."

"She's not here."

"Okay, does anyone still work for the police department that matters?" I was on a roll. "Detective Chico wasn't in today, either."

A chuckle.

"Pardon me?"

"They are in a scheduled meeting in Nashville," she replies. "Would you like an appointment to come in another day?"

"No, I'll take care of my problem on my own." I hang up.

I am seated in my Audi in front of Coffee Call and decide I need to pamper myself with something sweet alongside a cup of coffee.

As I enter the bistro I run straight into Gerry Bolton.

"Excuse me, Gerry, I didn't mean to bump into you."

"It's okay, Dorothy, I'm not all that fragile."

Well, I am, I think to myself. "Did you already have coffee?"

"No. I picked up some pastries for our kitchen staff at the Senior Citizen Center," he replies. "I never see you there anymore."

"I'm out of town a great deal." That's all he needs to know.

"Well, it's nice seeing you."

Is it? "Gerry, could I buy you a cup of Joe?"

He is surprised. No, amused.

"Sure, Dorothy. I can take fifteen." He grabs my elbow with his free hand and we march into the bistro. "Will this table do?"

"Perfect." I inhale deeply. I have questions for him.

"You don't have to avoid the Center just because of what happened with Gloria." He motions a server over to our table.

"I cannot tell you how sorry I am about Gloria, Gerry. We never saw eye to eye, but I never intended her harm." Guilt sloshes over me.

"We've already been down this road, Dorothy. . ." he places his hand over mine. "No hard feelings going forward, okay?"

"Thank you—I just received a gift in the mail for my birthday," my next thought spills out my mouth before I know it.

"What kind of gift?" H quirks his head to one side. Gerry is a good-looking man, more my age than Thomas is. *Focus, Dorothy.*

A server interrupts our conversation before I can answer.

"Dorothy? What do you want?" Gerry inquires.

"A hazelnut latte, hold the whip," I reply to the server.

"Black, straight up," he orders.

When the server is out of earshot, he leans forward. "Are you in danger, Dorothy? Why are you talking to me about a gift?"

I glare at him. "I suppose I want an outside opinion."

"From me?" He sits back, amusement in his expression.

"Well, since you took the place of Clint Howard, were you aware he was a CIA undercover plant?" I carefully observe his reaction.

"No, I wasn't, Dorothy. Was there a connection between you and Cint?" Our two coffees arrive at the table; mine lingers untouched.

He takes a huge sip. "Coffee's excellent."

I am uninterested in coffee at the moment.

"Clint was CIA, sent here to watch out for me."

A question lingers on Gerry's face as he ignores his coffee.

"My husband Arthur received a birthday gift from a man named Clyde Willems a few months before he was murdered—that was in October nearly three years ago. Are you certain you've heard nothing about this fiasco?" I query. "It was the start of my trouble, too."

"Positive," Gerry replies. "All of this is news to me."

"The name of the book Arthur received is *The Secret Garden.*"

"A well-known children's book. My grandkids have one," Gerry reveals. "That's truly a strange gift to give a senior citizen."

"Well, I never gave the book a second thought until Arthur was murdered and Clint Howard came into my life." *Like a tornado.*

I do not define details concerning our unorthodox relationship.

"Dorothy, I'd really like to hear more about this, but I'm on a short time leash. Would you like to get together later today?"

"Sure." I am not busy and I need an outside opinion regarding my problem. Which is—why am I in possession of this book?

"Let me buy your supper," Gerry suggests.

"Well . . ." I wonder how that will look. Will people think I am dating Gerry? That I offed his wife so I could be with him?

"We will be discreet, I promise." He grins at me. "Call it a business meeting. I can see you need a friend's opinion."

"Is that what we are now, friends?"

"I think we've been all along, just haven't acknowledged it."

"Okay. Why don't you call me with the details and I will meet you at the restaurant?" I have in mind to visit Alicia Colby today.

He gulps down his coffee and throws a twenty on the table.

"I invited you, let me pay."

"No, no, a gentleman never imposes upon a woman." He gets up. "By the way, you look great! What did you do to yourself?"

"A girl never tells her beauty secrets." I wink at him.

"You're too much, Dorothy. I'll see you later today."

It's not a date, I tell myself. Yet, it feels like one. *A real man,* not one in my dreams or in my foolish fantasies. Someone living here in Columbia that's flesh-and-blood with no agendas to trick me.

* * *

Alicia comes down on the elevator to greet me.

"Dorothy! Where have you been keeping yourself?" She hugs me tightly and drags me into a visitation room at the nursing-home facility.

"Well, a lot has happened, but I did not come here to complain."

"You did it, didn't you?" Alicia grins and the cracks in her face multiply substantially. She is ninety-three now, and fairly healthy.

"Yeah, I had a facelift in early June. When I look in the mirror I wonder if it's really me?" I chuckle. "I still have a few faint scars."

"You look twenty years younger than the last time we visited."

"Actually, so much has happened I feel twenty years older."

"That's not good." She motions me to the sofa.

I take a seat and hold her cold hands. "Have you made friends?"

"Oh, yes. Three other ladies and myself play Bridge every afternoon for a couple of hours before our evening meal," she replies.

"That's great! Whenever I am in town on Fridays, I either play Canasta with my friends at the Senior Citizen Center or watch them."

"What would we do without our friends?"

"I don't want to find out." Alicia lifts my mood like a cloud sliding away from the sun after it's rained. I won't share my troubles with her.

"How is the family that purchased my cabin?" she inquires.

"Ellie Simpson has had some problems with the woman's teenage boys." I think of the black man that showed up in the barn. *Dom.*

"Would you like a drink? We have a new coffee/tea bar."

"No thanks, I just had coffee with Gerry Bolton," I reveal.

"And he still speaks to you?" Alicia chuckles then coughs.

"He invited me to have supper with him tonight."

"And you're going? Why?"

I do not want to bother Alicia with my "book" problem, so I say, "I believe he's trying to make me feel better about Gloria's death."

"How does food make you feel better?"

That's a question I ponder also. Except, I know Gerry is smart, and I hope that he will have some insight into my predicament.

"We all have to move on with our lives, Alicia."

"Yes, we do. Look at me. I'm a great example."

"Are you sorry you moved to America?" She'd come to Columbia only to suffer grief. First, her great nephew Clyde Willems was murdered; then later on his sister Lorita. Like me, her life was in danger for a period of time. Mine still is. Hopefully, Alicia is safe now.

34

AT FOUR P.M., GERRY TEXTED me where to meet him for supper at 6 p.m. After visiting with Alicia Colby for an hour, I chose to spend the rest of the afternoon shopping for new clothes. Since losing forty pounds, I had dropped two pant sizes but only one in blouses.

Many truckers and farmers fraternize *The Last Stop* located at the intersection of Highway 64 and I-65. They come in here for a beer and sandwich before going home. I am only ten minutes late as I enter the dive and inhale the sumptuous food odors. Gerry is waiting for me.

"Sorry I'm late," I apologize. "Traffic was horrible."

"No problem, Dorothy," he says as we approach the counter.

He'd already told the cowgirl registering guests he needed a table for two, so a hostess sits us near a large window tucked in an alcove for privacy. Gerry slips her $10 for the trouble. I can't help but smile.

"You sure know how to win a girl's heart, Gerry."

"Now, do I, Dorothy?" he playfully replies.

I peruse the laminated menu with limited choices. Then I lock eyes with him. "Have you eaten here before?"

"No, but I've heard the sandwiches are good, so go for it."

Go for it. That was apropos, especially since I was about to spill my guts to a man I hadn't been around since high school. Knowledge can be both powerful and dangerous. I'm trusting him to be discreet.

"Did you have a nice day, Dorothy?" He sets his menu aside.

"I visited a friend and did some shopping."

"My wife enjoys—enjoyed the same things," he said.

"It's okay to talk about Gloria, you loved her very much."

"As you must have yours." It's a sober statement.

Let's get the chitchat out of the way, I am ready to plow on to a more serious conversation. "Can I ask you something?"

"Depends." He grins and I note a dimple in one cheek.

"How much do you know about my husband's death?"

"Arthur?" He quirks his head to one side. "I read about the two murders on Crystal Creek. If I'm not mistaken, a couple other related murders occurred. Not many details were given in the news media."

I nod. "Well, since all that happened two years ago, there have been many loose ends." I pause. "Apparently, I am one of them."

"Are you in danger, Dorothy?" He asks in a concerned tone.

"I have been for almost three years. I just didn't recognize it."

"Okay . . ." Gerry takes a moment to size up my situation. "What about Gloria? Was she targeted?" He waits for my opinion.

"No, I was the target. It just so happened I switched lattes with her. She took the bullet for me—so to speak. I'm so sorry."

We stare at one another for longer than I like.

"I know you said you forgave me," I remind him.

"Well . . ." Gerry shakes his head, "I can't fault you for trying to be nice to Gloria. I know you two were rivals in high school, but inviting her to join you and Lorene Perkins for coffee was a nice gesture. I think you were trying to make amends for past grievances."

"I was, honestly." His forgiveness touches me deeply.

"Everyone with eyes that see knew about your rivalry, Dorothy. You two were at each other's throats over what a guy might consider unnecessary," he recalls the past. "Look, you were both knockouts."

I smile at his description of me. "That's a lopsided compliment."

"I meant every word, and I mean it now. Nothing has changed. You are a beautiful, desirable woman even in your eighties." He grins.

"Thank you, Gerry."

"I presume you want to tell me something important, Dorothy."

"Yes, but what I reveal is for your ears only, are we clear?"

"Sure. You can trust me to be discreet."

"Okay, there have been two more attempts on my life since Gloria died from drinking the latte meant for me," I begin. "The gas range leak at Lorene Perkins' house was not an accident. Someone intended to blow us to Kingdom Come but failed since Sam Perkins entered the house first and detected the problem. Otherwise, I wouldn't be here."

Gerry reaches across the table and grasps my hand.

"Go on. Tell me more."

"Last week, the brake line on my BMW was cut," I reveal. "If a young guy had not stolen it, I would be the one they found lying in a ditch dead," I tell him. "Then there is this suspicious black man I saw in Ellie Simpson's barn. Oh, and a young man has been watching me."

"Have either of the men tried to hurt you?"

"No." I wonder if my imagination is out-tracking my mind.

He sits back, alarmed. "Have you told the police all of this?"

I nod. "They're trying to solve the murders, but so much is still unknown, Gerry. I am just trying to stay breathing through all of this."

"What about Witness Protection?"

"No, I won't do that. I won't hide for the rest of my days." I won't say years, because I'm pretty sure I don't have that long.

The silence between us lingers until our server appears. We both order deluxe burgers with salty fries and Coca Colas. For the next few minutes, I hear from Gerry about his life and what has happened since Gloria's death. When we've finished our meals, he pays our tab.

We go outside together into the darkness. The June evening is humid and too warm, but the breeze is pleasant as floral odors attach and blow across the countryside. "I need to show you something."

"What?" He walks me to my car.

"Not here. Can we go somewhere private?" I reply.

"Sure, follow me. I have a condo on the outskirts of Columbia." He opens my car door for me. "I promise no hanky-panky."

I slap his arm. "Did I say I didn't want hanky-panky?"

We both laugh and he knows me well enough to assume I am teasing. But to be honest, I would not mind a guy like Gerry in my life—but not until I've washed Thomas Kessler right out of my hair.

Gerry's condo is a two-bedroom flat with a concrete yard surrounding it. The kitchen-den combo is spacious, and there is a half bath off the hallway leading to the master suite. All in all, I estimate sixteen-hundred-square feet—tall ceilings, some fourteen-feet high. That makes it harder to heat and cool, but enlarges the spaces.

"This is lovely," I tell him after he's shown me through. "Are you leasing or purchasing?" I inquire, nosy me. Is he staying or leaving?

Should I stay or go? I think of a popular TV ad for a motel chain.

"I want some coffee?" he says as we enter the kitchen proper.

"Do you cook for yourself?" I open cabinets, nosy me.

"Sometimes. My mother was a great cook. After she died in her early forties from breast cancer, I sometimes cooked for Dad. He had favorite dishes you can't get in a restaurant. I was divorced by then."

"I knew Gloria was not your first," I tell him as I lean against the bar and watch him pour water in the Keurig Coffeemaker. There are international coffee inserts from all over the world stacked in a holder.

"Gloria actually is my third wife, as I was hers. We were happy."

I won't quiz him on two failed marriages.

"I could see how much you cared for Gloria when you first returned to Columbia to run the Senior Citizen Center."

"You can't hide love." He's so right; I think of Tom.

"Why did you decide to move back to Columbia?"

"Seems a lot of us return to our roots," he answers.

"Tennessee has always been my home. But I have no desire to return to Dickson. I've lived in Columbia most of my adult life."

"I think it's in our DNA to return to our roots, our homes, near the end of our lives. That's why it's called 'The Circle of Life'."

I smile as my coffee spews out of the machine. "I like that."

We sit at the kitchen bar and drink our coffees. Mine is loaded in cream but I left off the sugar. I don't want to gain pounds back.

"What did you want to show me?" He reminds me why I am here.

I grab my purse and remove the children's book I received by mail for my birthday. It is the same one Clyde Willems gave Arthur.

"There are details about Clint Howard you should know. His real name is Thomas Kessler." I remind him Tom works for the CIA.

Gerry has no comment so I continue my saga.

"Clint/Thomas volunteered to keep an eye on me after the CIA arranged for the serial killer, Mark Hagen, to escape from a Tennessee federal prison," I say. "He became my friend, or so I thought."

Gerry sips on his coffee as I give him an overview of why Tom volunteered to keep me safe. I look like his murdered wife.

"That's some drama, Dorothy. I had no idea."

"Most people don't, Gerry. But this book . . ." I pound it with my right hand, "holds many secrets. I think something has been added since last fall when I examined it." I look at him. "I'll show you."

I point out the circled words in the book and explain how it was decoded by a friend of Tom's and revealed the names of Russian Mafia bosses in four states. "This book was mailed to me last week."

"Why?"

"A birthday gift. No name attached. I opened it in front of my family on Sunday and was astounded—no shocked. The only thing that makes any sense is that Tom sent it to me."

"Have you figured out why?"

"No. I thought he died from a bullet wound last year when the feds rescued me from a Mafia safehouse on the outskirts of Crossville. I was being held hostage by a serial killer—that's another story."

"Goodness, Dorothy! You seriously live a complicated life."

"Tell me about it." I nervously chuckle over his comment.

We glare at one another before I continue. "The Christmas card I received from Russia this past December had to be from Tom."

"So, he's alive," Gerry concludes. "What are you thinking?"

"Look." I point out the circled numbers on specific pages in the book. These are new additions. I wrote them down in sequence."

I hand Gerry the paper with the numbers and he peruses them.

"In sequence, this could be a banking number."

My mouth drops open but no words come out.

"Do you have any idea which bank?" he queries.

"Maybe." I turn to the last page of the book and there are two capitalized letters that appear to be scratched by a child. KT.

"What do you think these letters means?" Gerry inquires.

"Possibly Knoxville, Tennessee," I reply.

"Okay." He places our coffee cups in the sink. "Let's go."

"Did you forget I have my own car?"

"You won't need it. You're coming with me."

35

Tuesday, June 27

CLAIRE'S CELL PHONE RINGS as she dresses June for her ballet class. Intelligent beyond her years, the five-year-old demands to be entertained every moment of the day. Her mother Helen is too busy with work to keep track of her two children. Presently, Billy is with his grandfather at the ballpark where junior baseball is in progress.

"Hello," Claire says to the caller. "Stand still."

"Pardon me?" quips the caller.

"Not you, sorry. I was talking to my granddaughter. Who is this?"

"Lorene Perkins."

"Oh, I didn't recognize your voice at first." Claire steadies June so she can complete her task. "Is my mother there with you?"

With one hand, Claire scoops June's long blond hair into a pony tail and secures it with a barrette. "Are you there, Lorene?"

"Yes. I thought Dorothy might be with you."

"No, it was my understanding she intended to stay in Columbia for a few more days—she left here with that odd birthday gift."

Lorene offers no solution to Dorothy's absence.

"You don't think something bad happened to Mama?" Claire's heart leaps at the thought of losing her mother at the hand of a killer.

"No, no, you know Dorothy. She probably spent the night with Ellie Simpson," Lorene speculates. "I'll give Ellie a call."

"Would you do that and text me when you find her," Claire says. "I have to get my granddaughter to her ballet class and run some errands." Ted and Billy were due home around eleven for lunch.

"Sure, Claire. No problem."

36

Wednesday, June 28

GERRY AND I SPENT the night at a Day's Inn in Knoxville. I had my own room, of course. I was already downstairs and waiting for him in the breakfast area off the atrium. The odor of sizzling pancakes on the griddle entices my appetite so I decide to splurge and enjoy some crisp bacon with two pancakes slathered in Maple Syrup.

While I am making a plate, Gerry enters the dining hall looking withered, like he'd been fighting the sheets all night. I wonder how he's coping over Gloria's death. It's only been three months since he buried her. I know I still think about Arthur a lot. My missing Tom, too.

"Good morning," I say as he approaches the breakfast bar.

"Yeah, it is." He grunts and heads for the coffee carafe. From observing his preference last night, I am not surprised he goes for the strong Columbian straight up. A real He-Man like Thomas.

Gerry is taller than Arthur was. Both were handsome teens. They played on the same high school basketball team for three years. Gloria and I were a couple of grades behind the boys, but like other dreamy girls we did not fail to notice their strong, rugged, athletic bodies.

Arthur dated Gloria first. It feels odd thinking of this now that she is deceased. Am I a bad person? True, I disliked her back then. And to be honest, I don't miss her much today. Shame on me!

"Penny for your thoughts!" Gerry brings me out of my revelry.

"Nothing important, just reminiscing."

"I do that often these days—thinking back on my high school and college days. I recall the good times mostly, but sometimes the awkward moments slip in," he reports as he sips on black coffee.

"What were you day-dreaming about, Dorothy?"

I look up at him hard. He shakes his head and smiles.

"Let's just focus on today, okay?" I tell him.

"Sure." He chuckles. "Private thoughts are just that; but answer me one question. Were you thinking about me?"

He's such a flirt. I won't answer him.

"Okay, what is on our agenda this morning?" he inquires.

"We need to decide which bank to visit first." I am all business.

"I already keyed in six major bank addresses," he informs me.

I join him at a table, feeling my stomach grumble.

"Before I see your information, I need to get some food first," I tell him and walk over to the long tables laden with breakfast choices.

After cooking two pancakes in the griddle, I pluck three slices of crisp bacon and add them to my plate before returning to the table.

"Aren't you going to eat something?" I ask.

"I need to wake up first, Dorothy. Not really a breakfast person."

"A night owl, I suspect. There are either morning persons or night persons—some say it's the time of day we're born," I utter.

"I was born just after midnight," he reveals.

"I think my birth fell in the middle of the day."

"Now that we have that important information out of the way, let's take a look at the city map of Knoxville and decide the route we should follow." He opens a flat printed map on the dining table.

"You've already circled the streets." I am surprised.

"I did not succeed in business by being reticent."

He uses big words, too, I note. He's not only handsome, he's intelligent. And not at all like Arthur, who turned out to be more like a farmer than a business man. But I loved my husband with all my heart. And I miss him. But he isn't here. Neither is Tom.

Gerry is. I need to focus on my problem.

* * *

Lorene decides to drive over to Ellie's without calling first. She finds the young woman clipping fresh flowers in the garden spot back of the house. Coming here reminds her of all the times she visited Dorothy. A stab of nostalgia attacks her and tears cloud her gaze.

"Oh." Ellie erects her skinny frame. She'd lost weight since her fiancé was murdered last year on Thanksgiving Day. "I didn't hear my phone ring." She approaches Lorene, removing her garden gloves.

"I didn't call," Lorene says. "I'm looking for Dorothy."

"She's not here, Lorene," Ellie replies. "It's been a week since I've heard from her or seen her. Are you worried?"

"A bit, I guess." Lorene walks with Ellie toward the back porch.

"I didn't know she was in town." Ellie opens the screen door. "Do you have time for coffee? My body could sure use a nip."

Lorene grins. "I could use a nip of something stronger."

"I have Bourbon, if you'd like some."

Lorene throws a hand. "No, better not. I'm driving."

"Mom and Dad are traveling again, so I'm pleased you stopped by for a visit." Ellie removes her straw hat. "I'm bored."

"Are you thinking of working again?" Lorene inquires. "You could take up knitting; you certainly can afford to stay home."

"I'm not a crafty person," Ellie says. "I need to move forward with my life. Butch is not coming back, and he would not want me to grieve for the rest of my life. Working will be good for me."

"Will you go back to being a secretary?"

"No, I want to open my own secretarial business." She has in mind to rent out secretaries to businesses that cannot afford help fulltime. Growing businesses never seem to have enough employees.

"That sounds exciting." Lorene trails Ellie inside the house.

She sits at the breakfast bar while Ellie perks ground coffee in an old-fashioned stainless-steel percolator that was popular in the 1940's.

"My mother had a coffeemaker just like that one," Lorene notes. "Where did you get it?" The water rises in a metal stem and hisses.

"A new Retro shop opened in Columbia," Ellie says. "They sell all sorts of items from the 1940s through the 70s. It's a fun store."

"I'll have to take Dorothy there one day soon—when I find her."

Ellie leans against the counter. "You have no idea where she is?"

"Nope, she was supposed to spend last night with me. No show."

"Is that unusual?"

"For Dorothy? No, it's a common practice," Lorene answers.

"Then, you should not worry. She's somewhere on a mission."

"No doubt." Lorene hears the percolator hiss and pause.

* * *

Gerry had driven me to four major banks in Knoxville. The fifth was located downtown, a First Federal Bank. I venture inside alone and approach the counter. The lady asks if is she can help me.

I respond, "Maybe. I have a number either to a bank account or possibly a lockbox, but I'm not sure which it is," I tell her. "I think my sister banked here. She's deceased," I lie. "I am her executor."

God forgive me but this is a life-or-death situation.

"This is highly irregular, Miss." The clerk glares at me like I'm a criminal trying to steal someone's assets. "I'll get the bank manager."

"Thank you, I'll wait over there." I have my eye on a chair.

I only have to wait ten minutes before a tall, lanky man too young to be the manager of this bank approaches me. "Come with me."

I am shown into a private office where Mr. Smythe sits behind his wide desk and motions me to a chair in front of it. He plants his forearms on the desk, twists his lips to one side, and sniffles.

"I need to see your I.D.," he tells me.

I comply and he stares at me. "What is all this about?"

"You want the summary, or the whole shebang?"

"The summary is fine."

I go through the spiel Gerry and I cooked up, about my needing to access my dead sister's bank account in order to pay bills; except her legal files were destroyed in a housefire. I discovered these numbers scribbled in a notebook inside her purse, thinking that the sequence resembled a bank account. How could I know where she banked?

"Does she have an address in Knoxville?" he inquires.

"Not anymore; she's been comatose for a couple of years."

Pants on fire, I'm getting the hang of lying. God forgive me.

"I see."

I wonder if he really does. I evaluate what I should say next and his gullibility to believe me. His expression seems empathetic.

"I've tramped from bank to bank all morning trying to determine which one my poor sister used. Can you help me, Mr. Smythe?"

I hand him the numbers printed on a sheet of typing paper. He looks at them then looks up at me. "This appears to be a number for one of our bank deposit lockboxes," he reports. "Want me to check?"

"Would you mind?" I am hopeful of a successful ruse.

"Do you want to accompany me?"

"Thank you."

He leads me inside a fault and finds the right metal drawer.

"Look, I need to see inside the box before I turn anything over to you," Mr. Smythe tells me. "If I suspect fraud, I'm calling the police."

"I would expect no less." I heave a belabored breath.

The lockbox is opened and I glare at its contents. There is a small pocket-sized leather-bound book that contains a lot of numbers like the one I've given Mr. Smythe. I have no idea what it means.

"This is meaningless to me, Mrs. Powell," he says.

"Can I have the notebook?" I ask politely. "Perhaps my brother knows what these numbers mean. We have bills to pay."

He shrugs. "Let me photograph the book then you may have it."

"Sure, no problem." I like the idea of having a safety copy in case someone steals it from me or Gerry, or we both end up dead.

Walking out of the bank feels like freedom. It's sunny and hot and I'm hungry again. I find Gerry slumped over the steering wheel of his Ford Explorer, snoring. Poor guy did not get enough sleep last night.

"Wake up, Gerry, I'm back." I tap on the window.

"Huh, uh . . ." he sits up and assesses where he is. "Dorothy."

"All day long. I got the loot."

"What?" He acts as if he's not part of this sting.

"Open the door for me, Gerry."

I race around the front of his SUV and leap into the passenger seat. "See for yourself." I hand him the black book.

"All I see is a bunch of numbers," he says.

"This book contains dozens of numbers like the one decoded in the children's book. I think they are lockbox numbers from different banks." I wonder if that includes Switzerland and the Cayman Islands.

"Let's go home then."

I nod, agreeing with him, but have no idea what comes next.

He cranks up the motor and we drive out of Knoxville and ramp onto Interstate-40 headed west toward Nashville. I feel—I don't know—triumphant maybe? Success feels like winning a Gold Medal.

We are back at his condo by 4:30 p.m.

"Thank you, Gerry." I sit there, wondering what comes next.

"No problem, Dorothy." He exits his car on the driver's side, walks around the front, then opens the passenger door for me.

Such a gentle soul, I think to myself. *I've ruined his life.*

"Will you let me know what those numbers mean?" He closes the passenger door and leans against it, his gaze almost penetrating.

"Sure, as soon as I know." I am so grateful for his help I feel like planting a wet kiss on his lips. But somehow, I feel Gloria is watching.

"Don't be a stranger," he calls out as I walk to my Audi. "Friends can have supper together. It doesn't mean anything, honest to God."

I turn around and smile sweetly at him.

"We'll see." A date means something to me.

37

AS I LEAVE COLUMBIA I am betwixt driving back to Claire's or staying another night with Lorene. I need time to think about this treasure I've found. This book of numbers must be significant or Tom would not have mailed it to me. He trusts my ability to decipher a mystery.

And God knows to a fault I love one.

I have a sack with four barbeque sandwiches and a large package of salty chips sitting on the passenger seat. I did not want to return to Lorene's at suppertime without food in my hand. Sort of as a peace offering since I failed to call her last night and tell her where I was, or what I was doing. I know she will have a ton of questions. I do, too.

I tap on her front door and hear the patter of feet closing in. Cynthia opens the door. "Oh, Mrs. Perkins, is Mama expecting you?"

I smile. So, Lorene is Mama now.

"Is she home?"

"Of course, I'm home, Dorothy. Where else would I be?"

I lock my gaze on Lorene. She's upset with me. I understand, I would be upset with her if the shoe fit my foot—so to speak.

"Am I welcome or not?" I offer her the sack of food as a peace offering—not that the bargaining chip had ever worked on Lorene.

"Depends on what's inside that sack," Lorene qualifies.

"Four of Bart's barbeque sandwiches. A peace offering."

Cynthia stands behind her mother-in-law taking in our strange conversation. I see the pooch in her stomach and know she's hungry.

A baby on the way can do that.

"Come on in, Dorothy. I just made a pot of vegetable soup. We'll have your sandwiches with it." She leads the way through the foyer into the den and finally in the kitchen. Graham is there.

"Hi, Graham." I set the food sack on the bar.

"Something smells delicious," he comments.

"Bart's barbeque sandwiches," Cyn tells him.

"Soups ready, Mama, let's eat," he addresses Lorene.

I excuse myself to potty and wash my hands.

By the time I return, the food has been dispersed on the table so I fill the only vacant seat left. "Sorry I took so long."

We all bow our heads in expectation of Graham's blessing over our meal. "We're glad you're here, Dorothy, but you didn't have to bring food," Lorene says after he is finished with a lovely prayer.

"I know, but I didn't want to crash in on you at suppertime since I failed to call in advance." I add barbeque sauce and slaw to my sandwich. "I hope all of you have had a pleasant day."

"I've been pretty maxed out with processing corpses," Cyn says.

I truly wish she had not brought up that subject—not over a delicious meal that I am about to share with good friends.

"Pharmacy business is booming—Covid tests sales and meds to minimize the infection. Million-and-a-half tested positive yesterday."

I despise bad news and that is all that's being served.

"Well, I had a pretty good day," Lorene chimes in. "I had a faucet leak in my master bedroom and Jeffery Tombs came to fix it."

"The widower?" Cyn perks up. "I just got his wife's body in port yesterday. I'm surprised he is working under the stress of grief."

"I don't think he's grieving much, Cyn. I heard he didn't get along with Sylvia at all. In fact, they have been separated for over a year."

Why did Lorene have to go and say that? Too much disturbing information at the supper table. I'm getting indigestion over thinking about dead bodies, Covid tests, leaky faucets, and unhappy marriages.

"What about you, Dorothy?" Graham asks, pointing a finger.

"Me?" I smile. "It's a perfect ending for the day. Sitting here with good folks like you around the supper table, I have no complaints."

By the time Lorene and I have cleaned the kitchen, the newlyweds have already gone upstairs for the night. I can only imagine what they are doing. Two lovers, expecting their first child? What a night!

"I talked to Claire and she's worried about you," Lorene says as she hangs the dishtowel on a door rack under the sink. "Where have you been staying? Not with your daughter or Ellie Simpson."

"Are you my sister's keeper, Lorene?" I glare in protest.

"No, but it's rude not to call when you're expected to spend the night," Lorene expresses concern. "I almost called the police."

"I'm glad you didn't. I was caught up in some urgent business I didn't think you, Claire, or Ellie needed to know about."

Lorene limps into the den and collapses in the recliner. I trail her and park my weary butt on the sofa. "I am truly sorry, Lorene."

"You are always sorry, Dorothy. Yet you repeat the same patterns. It's all about *you* and how *you* feel, and *your* agendas!"

Wow! I never expected that coming from my best friend.

"I would say that's mean, except you are right, Lorene. I have been preoccupied with my own troubles and left you out. I'm so sorry."

"Sorry doesn't cut it, my friend. I want the truth."

I know she does because she holds the TV remote and the TV is not on. It's time for *Survivor*, a program we both love to watch.

"If I tell you, will you promise not to tell Claire?" I inquire.

"Okay." Lorene's feet plop to the floor. "Is it a secret lover?"

I actually laugh. "If you call Gerry Bolton that. Yeah, I guess."

"You spent the night with Gerry? Gloria's husband?"

"Not anymore, he's a free agent now—like the athletes that play football. Gerry can go anywhere he wants, do anything, and live his life like everyone else should: minding their own blame business!"

Lorene's countenance plummets. I have wounded her.

"I know . . ." I calm down. "He's helping me with a problem."

"Why didn't you say so?"

"I'm saying so now."

"What kind of problem?" Lorene perks up.

"Can we make fresh coffee? I need caffeine. It's a long story."

"Sure, I have all night."

Two hours later, after I have finished with "The Saga of Dorothy Powell" Lorene's eyes are as big as bell peppers. "You don't say?"

"Now, I just need to figure out what all these numbers mean."

"How will you do that?"

"I'm going to Washington D.C. to speak with the CIA Director. Maybe he knows what all these numbers mean. Maybe, when I understand why the Russian Mafia wants me dead, I can sleep better."

38

Thursday, June 29

I DECIDED NOT TO tell Claire about my D.C. trip. I had Lorene's son Sam book me a round trip ticket on Thursday. I would have gone sooner but all the flights to Washington were filled. Only because of one cancellation was I able to get a seat. And it was costly.

Lorene drove me to the Nashville International Airport. The look on her face reflected concern and disgust. "What?" I look at her.

"I used to think you were nuts, Dorothy, now I know for sure."

I exit the Tesla and grab my overnight bag from the backseat. Then tuck my head inside the car again. "I'll be home late Saturday. Will you be here to pick me up? You have my flight info."

Lorene nods, gazing though tears while bent over the steering wheel like an old woman. She seriously needs to hire Dr. Sharra.

"Thank you. I'll phone as soon as I land," I tell my friend.

"If you don't keep your promise, Dorothy, I'll call Detective Chico and put her on your trail. Are we crystal clear?"

I snuggle a smile, proud of Lorene's bold remark. "We're clear." I shut the passenger door and turn away to fulfill my destiny.

The airport concourse is crowded with passengers coming and going. In our spirited world, one can travel anywhere in a pretty short time compared to the old seafaring vessels our ancestors manned.

I am at the Delta Counter twenty minutes before boarding. My cell phone dings before I have a chance to silence it for the flight.

It's Claire. I have to take this. And lie like a pro.

"Mama?" she begins. "I expected you home before now."

"Did you forget tomorrow is my day to play Canasta with the girls?" I think telling the truth is better than outright lying.

"I did not forget. I talked to Lorene and she didn't know where you were," Claire offers. "Where exactly are you, and what is that background noise? It sounds like you are in a crowd of people."

"I am. Everyone seems to have an agenda. I need to purchase some items for myself—I've lost weight, as you have obviously noticed." That is not a lie, so I am one-hundred percent on target.

Truth shall set you free, I recall a Bible scripture.

"Okay," Claire says. "Enjoy your shopping spree, and I will see you at my house on Saturday." She waits for my confirmation.

"Okay, but it might be late in the day. I have to deliver an item to a friend in Columbia before I make the drive to Nashville."

This is the truth. Simply because if I get answers that help me understand what the numbers recorded in the small book I confiscated from the Knoxville Federal Bank mean, I will be knocking on Detective Chico's door with a report that will knock her socks off.

"Okay, Mama. I don't pretend to understand what drives you to madness, but I accept your promise since I have no other choice."

I chuckle to myself. "I love you, Claire. You are the best."

"Well, that's something." She ends the call.

Is she mad at me, or just frustrated?

"If you are elderly, or handicapped, you may board now," a voice calls out over the intercom system. I step up and get in line.

The flight is full. Passengers are masked since airlines require it as a health precaution. A flight attendant reviews the safety rules as the pilot backs away from the airport. We turn and drift along until the tower gives our pilot permission to take off. The bird lifts off the tarmac in a V formation and my stomach reacts. I am both excited and fearful of what atrocities I will unmask tomorrow.

God help me be strong if the opposition turns nasty!

* * *

"Were you just talking to your mother?" Ted inquires. His bruises and cuts have minimized and he's feeling pretty good about the insurance payout on his Mercedes Benz. "Did you tell her?"

"No, she'll be home late Saturday," Claire replies.

"I think she'd want to know that Billy has been hospitalized with complication to Covid 19," Ted offers. "You should call her back."

"No, I do not want to upset her. Billy's pediatrician has assured Helen and Patrick that he will be fine with treatment and oxygen."

Ted lets go of a breath. "We don't know much about how this virus works in children. I told Helen he should be vaccinated."

"What about the side effects of heart issues and damage to his gonads?" Claire poses. "He might not be able to have children."

"He might not grow up to have children if he dies," Ted says.

"Oh, honey, please don't voice that. I know God loves Billy and will take care of him. If he's worse tomorrow, I'll call Mama back."

Ted doesn't answer Claire as he ventures into the backyard. He has yet to tell her he's divorcing her to marry his pretty assistant. Natalie is fifteen years younger and loves him despite his faults. How can he turn down such a smart desirous woman? Claire will be fine.

Divorces happen all the time. But since Billy is sick, he will delay the news. It's not the time to place an unnecessary burden on Claire. Besides, he's paying for Natalie's rent in a new high-rise apartment complex, and she seems content to see him a couple of nights a week.

39

TOO LATE IN THE DAY to show up at the Pentagon, I had no intention of announcing in advance that I was coming. If the front desk clerk, or guard, tried to stop me from seeing the CIA Director, I plan on creating a scene that would for sure get his attention.

The weather is overcast with heavy clouds so dusk will cloak the city early. I instruct the Uber driver to drop me off at the nearest hotel or motel to the Pentagon. The soccer mom lets me off in front of a three-story, yellow stucco-sided hotel. Considering its weathered roof tiles, the late-sixties-built hotel was not my first choice, but would have to do. I grabbed my overnight bag and entered the foyer.

I lock my gaze on the slouchy male with marble-size blue eyes like ice cubes and wonder how he landed a front-desk job.

"Do you have a reservation, Miss?"

Miss? I already like this quirky guy.

"No, I don't. Is there a room available?"

He jacks up his loose trousers with a hand and snorts, "We always have a room or two left. Name and I.D." He holds out a calloused hand that tells me he works a different day job. This is for extra money.

I present my driver's license and pay cash for the room. $200. They ought to outlaw businesses for robbing out-of-towners.

My room is located on the third floor. I step into the vault of an old-fashioned elevator with two mirrored sides and tile squares on the others. The ride up is slow and the machinery creaks like it's on is last leg. Like me, I suspect. Then get off in a long hallway that smells like stale tobacco and spilt alcohol despite the potpourri carpet cleaner.

Room 308 feels clean and I'm grateful. I toss my overnight bag on a fabric stool and set my purse on the round table crammed against the window AC that's working overtime. I respect anything that does.

I sit down on the queen bed and stare out a large window. From here I can see the five-sided building where spooks dwell with other spooks trying to keep America safe through spying on other countries. Sometimes they spy on our people too. They have me, for a fact.

I wonder if Thomas Kessler has an office in the quarters of the Central Intelligence Agency. I hope Director Jackson Carlton is still in charge of the spy organization. I know he will recognize my name when I arrive at the downstairs desk tomorrow morning. I'm still speculating what I can say that will get me through the check point and up to his office. I hear a bleep on the phone. It's a text from Lorene.

I punch in her cell number and wait for her to answer.

"Dorothy Powell, you promised to call!" she lashes out.

"Hold your horses, that's what I'm doing now."

"Are you somewhere safe?"

"I'm at a motel, Lorene. Safe and sound."

"Not of mind," she teases.

"And your mouth needs a swab of soap."

"Do you have a plan yet?" Lorene asks.

"I'm working on it, but don't worry I always manage to let loose something stupid that's bound to get someone's attention."

"I believe that. What did you tell Claire?"

"How do you know I spoke to my daughter?"

"She called here first," Lorene replies.

"What did she want?"

"To speak to you, but I told her you'd gone shopping."

"Good girl, that's what I inferred when she called me at the airport before I boarded." I suddenly feel worn out. "Lorene, I'm tired."

"No doubt, lying takes a lot of effort."

"I didn't lie, I just did not tell the whole truth."

"Same thing—news media does it all the time," she hails.

I laugh. "I know why I like you so much, Lorene. Two minds like ours run in the same gutter. It's refreshing to have a partner in crime. I hope you never find someone more devious than me."

"Well, put like that, I think you are safe."

"Okay, I need to take a nap then find a joint where I can have some supper. Then I'll lay out a plan for tomorrow. Pray for me?"

"I will, but if you lie to Jesus—"

A Latte to Die For

"Don't even think that, Lorene," I cut her off. "I'll phone you tomorrow after I've committed a crime and the CIA Director arrests me. I sincerely hope I get my one call and that hasn't changed."

"Shouldn't it be to Claire?" Lorene asks.

"Heaven's no! I don't want to lie to her again."

40

Friday, June 30

THE MONTHS OF APRIL, June, September, and November have thirty days. February has either twenty-eight, except every four years on what's called a leap year, in which case there are twenty-nine days.

I do not know why that seems important as I take a city cab over to the Pentagon. Somehow, I feel like the end of April is the leap I am about to take that will finalize the last nail on my coffin. Unless I am cremated, which seems to appeal more to me than resting six feet deep in the ground. I am bound to get lonely. And I've had enough of that.

I am wearing a blue teal suit with a pair of new black pumps. I am five-feet ten inches tall and weigh 140 pounds. My face has less wrinkles than it did a month ago. And the new Cover Girl makeup on my face hides any leftover red marks or scars from my surgery.

I am dressed and ready for war as I walk through the front door of the Pentagon. A nice soldier with good hair stands guard. I feel his eyes on me as I pass him and nod, as if I belong here, as if I am someone important like a Senator or a member of a Congressional Committee. I read about all that last night. Dr. Google, my friend.

"Do you have an appointment?" the female officer in the glassed-in kiosk asks me. "I'll also need to see some identification."

"No appointment, but Director Carlton is expecting me."

It's only a little white lie. When he learns what I have in my purse, he will be anxious to talk to me. "Call him," I order her.

"Your name, Miss?"

Miss? Do these people think I am young? If they do, they are not very smart and our country is in big trouble. "Dorothy Powell."

I wait while the sergeant, or whatever rank she is, calls up to the CIA office. I don't know how all this works, but I've prayed to God for favor. All I want is for the truth to come out, and to be safe again.

"He's sending someone down to talk to you."

"Thank you." I glance around to decide where best to wait.

"Oh, Miss? There's a lounge to your left. Wait there."

"Yes, thank you." I cross the spacious corridor and enter a cordoned off space where guests wait. I am not alone. Three uniforms sit across from me, two of them dozing. I peruse a magazine, mostly with advertisements and a splattering of articles that describe the workings of the U.S. Congress. I toss the magazine and sit on the sofa.

I don't have to wait long. A man in his late fifties with poignant green eyes and good hair stands in the opening. It seems everyone important has good hair. Maybe it's a governmental requirement. Do more people vote for politicians that have good hair? Arthur never would've made it in politics; certainly not in Washington D.C.

"Mrs. Powell?" the tall man addresses me.

Are all CIA agents tall? Or is it my imagination? Thomas Kessler was tall, six-feet five at least. This agent rivals his height.

"Yes, I'm Dorothy." I unsteadily stand up.

"What is your business with the Director?" he inquires.

"My business." I will not be bullied.

He smiles. "Tom said you were a handful."

"You know *my* Tom?" I immediately regret my statement.

"Your Tom." He grins. "That tells me a lot, Dorothy."

I feel my cheeks flush. I am no match for this agent.

"Is he here?" I dare ask, my blood pressure increasing a notch. I both want to see him and shoot him at the same time. I love him. Love does terrible things to a woman who feels spurned.

"No, he's not. Do you know where he is?"

I inch closer to him. "Now, that tells me something, too, Agent Whoever-You-Are." This game just etched up a notch.

"Charles Darby. My pals call me Charlie." He escorts me across the atrium toward a bank of elevators. I don't like manhandling.

"Is that what I am, Agent Darby? Your pal?"

He stops walking and glares down at me.

"Why are you here, Dorothy?"

"To see Director Carlton. I have information that will clear up a lot of questions surrounding the murders in my hometown," I reply.

"Columbia, Tennessee." Charlie nods. "Director Carlton is busy. I'm afraid you've wasted a trip. Come back tomorrow."

"Maybe you can help me." I'm not giving up the ship.

He removes a cell phone from his pocket and keys in some secret-agent message. His forefinger up signals for me to wait.

I am usually not a patient woman, but I somehow believe I have won this stand-off and am about to face off with the Director.

* * *

Ted came home from work early on Friday. He'd spent the morning in bed with Natalie. Walking around to the backdoor, he'd hoped to avoid Claire. But she was in the backyard pushing June in the gym-set swing. Billy was still hospitalized but doing better.

He heads for the back porch.

"Hi, honey, did you get lunch?" Claire calls out to him.

"Oh, hi. Sorry, I didn't see you there." He is lying through his teeth. What can a cheating husband do otherwise?

"I had plenty to nourish me this morning." He kisses Claire on the cheek, secretly savoring his clever answer to her question.

"June, let's go inside and I'll feed you lunch," Claire calls out.

"Have you spoken to your mother today?" Ted opens the backdoor for Claire. June squeezes between them and goes in first.

"No, but I've left two messages on her cell. She's probably at the Senior Citizen Center having lunch. It's her day to play Canasta with her friends." Claire widely yawns as the porch door snaps shut.

"You look tired, dear. I think our daughter expects too much from you. If she and Patrick need to work so many hours, they should hire a nanny, or put their children in a day school." They go in the house.

"I know, but I'd rather look after them. The world is too evil, and creeps tend to prey on innocent children. We don't want that."

Ted sets his briefcase on the floor and unloads his pants pockets.

"No, we don't want that. But Claire, you need to think about the next stage in your life. Now that the kids are grown, what do you want to do with your time?" Ted hopes to entice her to jumpstart a career.

Claire plops down in a barstool to consider Ted's question. She shrugs. "I don't know. So far, I have a very busy life."

"With June's children and your mother—that's not a life."

He studies Claire. She is still a lovely woman and super smart. She will be fine without him. That is if he decides to marry Natalie.

"I need to feed June lunch and rest," she tells Ted.

"MG, can I have a peanut-butter and jelly sandwich?"

"Sure." Claire hops off the barstool to fix June's lunch.

Ted grabs her arm. She laughs. "What's with the manhandling?"

"This is important, Claire. You studied to be an interior decorator in college, don't you want to open up your own business?"

She hitches a hand on one hip. "Have you been drinking?"

"No." He frowns. "Don't change the subject to me. Look, we can afford for you to be fulfilled as a whole person."

"I am fulfilled, Ted. I have you, and I have a wonderful family. And I still have my difficult mother I love dearly."

He shakes his head. "I need a glass of water. Can I get you something to drink?" He walks over to the refrigerator.

Claire makes June's sandwich and helps her mount the barstool. She pours herself a glass of tea and gives June a cup of milk.

Ted kicks off his loafers as he pads barefoot over to the sofa with a tall glass of ice water. It won't be easy leaving Claire for Natalie.

41

DIRECTOR CARLTON'S OFFICE IS impressive. I take a seat in front of his desk and wait for him to make a dramatic entrance.

Isn't that what important people do?

But he doesn't come in. Charlie does.

I lean slightly forward. "I don't understand."

"What evidence are you carrying in your purse, Mrs. Powell?"

"I thought we were friends. I thought I was Dorothy to you."

"Not anymore, this is business," Charlie tells me.

"Where is Director Carlton?"

"Out for the day. He left me in charge."

"Can I trust you?"

"I am the damn CIA, what do you think?"

"I think there is more going on in this office than anyone lets on," I unsteadily stand up. "I will call him tomorrow. I'm leaving."

He gets up and closes the door. "I don't think so."

"I'll scream for help!" I warn him.

"Soundproof room; won't help you."

"What am I missing?" I ask, totally confused. The best-made plans don't always pan out, I recall once thinking. And I was right.

He walks over to me and takes my purse. "Let's have a look."

"Give that back!" I struggle with him for my purse and lose.

"Mrs. Powell, Dorothy, relax. I just need to see what evidence you have that you deem so important to show up in D.C. and ask to speak to the Director." He empties the contents of my purse out on the desk and thumbs though my incidentals. Lipstick, tissue, ballpoint pen. Compact. "What's this?" He holds up the small black book.

"It's what I wanted to show the Director."

He thumbs through the book and looks at the numbers.

"Do you know what those numbers mean?"

I do not like the expression on his face.

"Why don't you wait outside the office while I make a few calls?" He opens the door for me. "I won't be long. Have a seat."

I'm grateful he didn't pull a gun on me. Charlie has a baby face but doesn't fool me. He's not at all like my Tom. I don't trust him.

The door closes and I sit down to think this through. Where is everybody? Where are the other agents? What am I missing? All these questions make me extremely nervous. But I wait, no other choice.

Charlie opens the door sooner than I anticipate.

"Okay, Mrs. Powell, you can leave now. I'll keep this book with me and see that Director Carlton gets his hands on it."

I wobble to my feet. "No, I'll take it with me."

"Okay." He hands me the book. "Have a good day."

I'm on the elevator and on my way down to the atrium wondering what just happened. Charlie let me go too easily. I must be missing a piece of the puzzle. But, at least, I still have my little black book.

* * *

My plane landed in Nashville on time at 4:35 p.m. The weather in Tennessee had turned hot and nasty in the past twenty-four hours.

As I exit the airport through automatic doors, I hear thunder rumbling overhead as storm clouds gather. After returning to the hotel in Washington long enough to pick up my overnight bag and check out, I had cabbed over to the D.C. International Airport and checked in at the gate to await my flight. Which was at 3 p.m.

Now, I am back. Like the Terminator, only clueless of my mission at this point. I feel raindrops on my face as I glance around. With no parking available, I watch as cars circle through the driveway to pick up passengers. Lorene's Tesla does not appear. Gerry Bolton's SUV does. He pushes open the passenger door. "Get in, Dorothy."

Never one to contest a handsome man, I toss my overnight bag in the backseat and climb aboard. "Is there something I should know?"

"Yeah, Lorene phoned. Cynthia had a bleed and Graham was working, so she took her to the hospital." He drives out of the airport proper and connects with I-40 going west. "So . . . D.C.?"

"So, I took my little black book to the Pentagon, got in far too easily, and was hijacked by a CIA agent named Charles Darby. He told me to call him Charlie. All his friends do." I take in a huge breath.

"Then what's wrong, Dorothy? You don't look pleased."

"I'm not," I tell him as he passes a truck hauling a long line of new cars far too fast, which reminds me I am in the fast-lane of discovery now, and it occurs to me that my life is probably in more danger.

"Is it something you can share?"

I like Gerry. He's easy to talk to, and has no agenda as far as I can discern. In fact, he should despise me for my part in his wife's death. I know he loved Gloria very much. Why wouldn't he? She was beautiful, intelligent, and socially polished in every way possible.

He looks over at me as we ramp off 440 onto I-40 again.

"I trust you more than most people, Gerry."

He smiles at my statement.

"Director Carlton was not in his office, so Agent Darby invited me up to their headquarters. We were the only ones there."

Hmmm, he grunts. "Did that seem odd?"

"Very, and he made me feel uncomfortable," I recall. "He insisted I show him what I'd brought to the Director that was so important."

I pause to reflect on our conversation.

"He emptied the contents of my purse on his desk, took my book, then told me to wait outside. He shut the door," I inform Gerry. "But I wasn't left alone for very long. The whole scene seemed odd."

"Why did he want to be alone in the office?"

"He said to make a few calls; I presume to Director Carlton."

"And then he comes out to talk to you again?"

"Yes. He said I could leave, but he was keeping the book to show to Director Carlton." I am still trying to figure out the logistics.

"What did you do then?" Gerry queries.

"I said no, that I'm keeping the book."

"Did he give it back to you without an argument?"

"Yes, and then I left the Pentagon."

Silence sliced through the air between us.

"You don't understand why he gave up the book so easily."

"It makes no sense at all," I conclude.

Gerry grins then chuckles as he pounds the steering wheel.

"Wait! You think you know why?" I am on the edge of my seat with the seatbelts holding me back like huge hands.

He shakes his head. "Dorothy, he copied the book."

Huh?

"He took pictures of the pages with his phone," Gerry speculates. "He didn't need your book anymore. He has the information."

I sit back and let the seatbelt cradle me like a baby. I can't move. Yes, I got the information where it needed to be. But did I give it to the right person? I don't know *this* Agent Charlie Darby. And I don't trust him. I wish that I could speak with Tom about what happened.

"Your silence tells me you are troubled," Gerry notes.

I release a labored breath. "Well, there is really nothing else I can do but take this hot little item to Detective Chico."

"I think that's wise, but it's Saturday. Give me the book for safekeeping and I'll lock it up in my safe at the condo. You can pick it up on Monday and go over to the police precinct. I'll go with you."

"What about your job?"

"It's not as important to me as your safety, Dorothy."

"You are so sweet, Gerry. I never expected this, not in a million years." I reach over and grasp his hand and tingles trickle through me.

Gerry is here, Tom isn't.

42

GERRY LETS ME OFF at Claire's house in Brentwood. It's closer to six p.m. since Gerry and I stopped for coffee. He wanted me to set some safe goals for myself, in case my information given to the CIA went sideways. I am becoming quite efficient with police lingo. *Sideways*.

Claire is in the home office typing on her computer.

"Hi, Love, I'm back." I do not say home because this residence is not my permanent one. Still, I need to decide what home is for me.

"Hi, Mama." She glances up at me and stops typing.

"Am I interrupting something important?" I inquire.

"No, I was investigating the possibility of opening a business." She stands and stretches. "How was the Canasta game?"

"Fine." My replacement did well, I'm sure.

"Did you take care of personal business today?"

Claire asks too many questions. I'm proficient at bending the truth some of the time, but not always. I want to share with her what happened in D.C. but, if I do, she will go ballistic and accuse me of being nuts. She might even have me locked up so I'll see a psychiatrist with the capability of rewiring my brain. Good luck with that, Love!

"I'm tired, Claire, do you have plans for supper tonight?"

"No, Ted has a client he's wining and dining tonight."

"Why don't I treat you to a steak at Morton's?"

"Isn't that kind of expensive for your budget?"

"I'm not counting pennies, Claire. At my age, every day could be my last." I am not thinking of a natural death.

"Don't say that, Mama, it makes me sad."

"Is it a date?" I stand like a sentry in the doorway.

"I need to shower and change clothes first."

"Okay, you do that while I make a few calls."

"Mama, I did not tell you Billy was in the hospital because I did not want to worry you," Claire reveals. "He's doing much better."

I glare at my daughter. "You didn't think I could handle it."

She shakes her head. "I did not want to add to your burdens."

Now my family is protecting me from life. I am their failure.

While Claire retreats to her master bedroom suite to clean up and dress for our date, I phone Lorene. "Hi, it's me."

"Are you in Nashville?"

"Yes, I'm with Claire. We're going to Morton's Steakhouse for supper. Gerry told me Cyn had to be hospitalized."

"Her OBGYN is keeping her overnight for observation," Lorene replies. "I hope it was okay I asked Gerry to pick you up at the airport. You were still in flight when I hurried off to the hospital."

"It was fine. We had coffee before he brought me to Claire's."

"How was it, I mean, you know?"

"Yes, I know." I chuckle. She's referring to my visit to the CIA office. Lorene is really into all this clandestine stuff. I think she gets her thrills through me. Then I am taking all the risks. But not all of them. She's in danger because she's with me, on my side, my confident, and my best friend. We should get a permanent divorce.

"Let's just say, I was nearly successful," I tell Lorene.

"What does that mean?"

"Let's save this conversation for another time. I don't want to talk about it over the airways." One can never know if Big Brother is listening. I don't trust Agent Darby as far as I can throw him.

"Okay, will I see you on Monday—Oh, wait! We have an invitation to Ellie Simpson's 4th of July shindig. Jasmine and Wes are having the food catered from Bart's Barbeque. It should be fun."

"Sounds like a winner," I say as Claire enters the den. "I need to go now. I will see you soon. Bye, Lorene."

"How is she?" Claire asks, looking gorgeous in her green silk blouse and black pants. Her ruby-red hair is styled in a bob and I am drawn to her radiant blue eyes. She's a knockout. Ted's a lucky guy.

"Lorene is Lorene, but Graham's wife is in early pregnancy and had to be hospitalized. It's their first child, so Lorene is worried."

"Of course, she is. I remember when Helen was pregnant with Billy. Every time she had a stomach cramp, I wanted her to call her doctor. But everything worked out fine, and it will for Cyn, too."

"I love your optimism, Daughter."

"And I love you, Mama. Let's go pig out on steak."

"I'm with you."

We hook arms and march out the kitchen door into the garage and get into Claire's Buick and head off to the restaurant like Dorothy and her pals did in the Wizard of Oz. Life cannot feel much better than this. Me with Claire. Together, we'll conquer our problems.

43

Tuesday, July 4th

I WAKE UP IN LORENE'S bed and squint at the wall clock. Obviously, I need prescription glasses since my distant vision is not as good as it used to be. It's 7:10 a.m. We've slept in late. I nudge my bedfellow.

"What?" Lorene rolls over in the bed and faces me.

"Didn't you tell Ellie we'd we over early at her house to help set up for the picnic?" I crawl from the covers and feel my bones crunch. I may look much better on the outside, but what's inside is still aging.

Breakfast is a blueberry muffin with juice and coffee. I am okay with that after my huge steak dinner with Claire Saturday evening. It seemed odd to me that Ted did not get home before midnight. I wanted to ask Claire if things were okay between them, but didn't.

None of my business; I know the routine.

"Dorothy?"

"Were you speaking to me?"

"Yes. Where were you?"

"La-la Land, I suppose."

She chuckles. "You never explained what happened in D.C."

She's prying again. Better she doesn't know any details.

"It's complicated," I mutter. "Did you make the muffins?"

"Kroger Bakery, Dorothy. What's the big CIA secret?"

"I'd rather not discuss what took place at the Pentagon," I tell her. "Gerry is helping me discern how to resolve some issues."

"Now it's *issues* and not problems? No way."

Lorene says it like I have the plague and Gerry should be avoiding me at all costs lest he get caught up in my ongoing drama.

"Yes, way." I love teasing her.

"Did you sleep with him the night you disappeared?"

Lorene is on a roll and I don't want to disappoint her.

"If I did, I would not tell you. A girl has gotta have some secrets." I recall what I once told Claire: *What happens undercover stays there.*

Lorene's upper lip stiffens. "I know you didn't. You wouldn't."

"You mean after I murdered his wife." I am on a roll.

"I swear you can turn a conversation into a tsunami." Lorene pours herself a second cup of Joe and adds cream and two sugars.

"No, I did not sleep with Gerry. We had a nice conversation and I decided to tell him about my unusual birthday gift."

"You never told me about your unusual birthday gift."

"Well, it's not like I've had the chance, Lorene."

"Well, now is your chance."

"It's too complicated to go into all that right now. Let's get over to Ellie's house and help her set up for the picnic."

"Okay, I forgive you. But you will tell me about the gift?"

She is persistent, so I might as well get it over with.

"Don't move, I'll be back." I hold up a forefinger then return to the bedroom to fetch the small black book from my purse.

Lorene hasn't moved a hair since I departed.

"This book is a mystery." On Monday, I'd decided not to get the police involved. I still needed answers to what the numbers meant.

She opens the book and thumbs through the pages.

"All it has is random numbers. What do they mean?"

"Exactly my problem. That's why I flew to Washington, D.C., to get answers," I explain. "Only I got the shaft instead."

"I don't understand." Lorene's nose wrinkles.

"I got put off, shoved out, vamoose!"

"I know *vamoose;* it's quoted many times in western movies."

"Exactly. Get lost!"

In the next fifteen minutes, I would explain to Lorene how Gerry and I discovered a lockbox number of a bank in Knoxville, Tennessee.

"Last year, after Tom and I found the children's book Clyde Willems gave Arthur for his birthday before he was murdered, it had circled words. None of the page numbers were circled," I explain.

"And you wonder why?" Lorene posed.

"I presumed the page numbers were a clue to the mystery that been unravelling my brain for nearly three years."

"Well put, Dorothy." She chuckles.

"Thinking the numbers might be assigned to a money account or lockbox, Gerry drove me to Knoxville to find the bank," I continue.

"How did you know which bank?" Lorene asks.

"We didn't. Process of elimination."

Lorene thinks about all I have said.

"Did Tom send you the children's book?"

"It makes sense that he did," I conclude.

"I thought he gave it to the CIA for safekeeping," Lorene says.

"That would make better sense."

"So, maybe someone from the CIA other than Tom sent you the book," Lorene offers, chasing thoughts that keep flowing forward.

"That would complicate my sensibilities."

Lorene laughs at my joke. "You don't know who sent it."

"No, Lorene, I don't know."

"Why didn't you just say so?"

"You were having too much fun." I laugh.

She throws the book at me, literally.

* * *

"Where were you last night, Ted?"

He looks at his wife. "Claire, I already told you that I have several new clients who expect me to entertain them. They are singers and actresses and have busy schedules. It's my job, so you can enjoy your grandchildren and not work—unless you really want to," he adds.

"I've been thinking about what you said about fulfilling my own dreams," Claire tells Ted. "I'll need to take some refresher courses in Interior Decorating before I launch a business. That will take time."

He smiles. "Take all the time you need, Claire. I'll foot the bill; I just want you happy. And if a career makes you happy, I'll be happy."

Claire kisses him on the lips as he sits at the patio table sipping on a glass of O.J. "Are the kids coming over today?" he inquires.

"Did you forget? Helen is throwing a 4th of July party for the people she works with and we are invited. Shindig starts at 4 p.m."

44

ELLIE HAD ALSO INVITED Lorene's two boys. Graham came to the picnic with Cyn, who appears as fragile as breakable China. Every time she starts to get up for something, he intervenes and runs the errand for her. It is evident he was head-over-heels in love with her.

I thought about Arthur and how he would never be coming back; never put his arms around me again, and it makes me sad. Then there was my dreamboat, Thomas Kessler. There was a time when I knew him as Clint Howard and hoped that we could weather time together.

But that did not work out, either. And now there is Gerry Bolton waiting in the wind—so to speak. We are at least friends.

"Dorothy?"

"If you say 'penny for your thoughts', Lorene, I swear I will clobber you!" I am mad she's pulled me from my thoughts of a better future. Not every woman my age gets that chance, even in a daydream.

"I wasn't going to say that at all!" Lorene takes exception. "The food is ready to be served. Ellies wants us to help her."

"Sorry, I'm a bit jumpy today." I don't know why, but something is stirring in the wind, and it is not good, at least not for me.

It's the hair raised on my spine, a prehistoric sense of foreboding, or something like that. I cannot explain it. But trouble is on the way.

Lorene's younger son Sam arrives late with his girlfriend, Darla. She'd moved to Columbia at the beginning of the high-school's spring semester to substitute teach History for Joel Henderson when he contracted Covid and was hospitalized. He didn't make it.

His funeral was in March. A very sad occasion.

After everyone is served barbeque sandwiches, baked beans, salty chips, and colas, Ellie's guests find seats in the backyard. Wes had arranged for a jazz band to entertain us. The weather is spectacular today for early July. Sunny, low humidity, the temp about 88 degrees.

While Lorene talks with Jasmine, I see Sam's date heading over my way. I brush the crumbs off my lap and set the paper plate on the ground. "Mrs. Powell," Darla says, "I wanted to meet you," she tells me. "You've made an impression on Sam; he speaks well of you."

"He does?" I know I am a deep subject, but I bet Darla has gotten an earful concerning my past shady shenanigans.

"I hope you have enjoyed your stay in Columbia, will it be permanent—I mean, will you continue with your teaching job?"

"Yes, especially now that Sam and I are dating."

"I have to say he has the eye for a pretty girl, and you certainly fit the bill, Darla. Down deep, I bet you are smart and courageous."

"I am. Sam's a firefighter, and I like to put out my own fires."

And start them, too, I think. I bet they already sparked.

"I heard Ellie's property once belonged to you," she says.

"Yes, my husband Arthur and I lived here five decades." I will not mention he was murdered; she probably already knows that.

"It's a lovely home. I want to take a walk by the creek before Sam and I leave," she tells me. "I bet you miss living here."

"I do, but my memories of this house are not all good. There comes a time when we all must open a new chapter to our Book of Life." I think of two important books safely tucked in my big purse.

Darla smiles. "That's a nice way to put it, Mrs. Powell. I lost someone I loved very much last year—my mother. She died from ovarian cancer. Doctors did not diagnosis it in time to save her."

"The silent killer, I've heard."

"My dad is still grieving. Maybe if he comes for a visit, you can have coffee with him. I think it would help to know someone else has gone through grief. What do you think?" She looks at me.

"I would be honored, Darla. I'm back and forth between Columbia and Nashville where my daughter Claire lives. You'd need to give me some notice." I abandon the lounge chair and stretch.

"It was nice talking to you. I'll get your cell phone number from Ms. Lorene when I know for sure my dad is coming for a visit."

"You do that, and have a great day!"

"Thank you. You, too."

I glance around for Lorene and do not see her anywhere. Perhaps, she went inside the house. Anyway, I want to take a long walk and stretch my legs and work off all the calories I just piled in my belly.

Before I know it, I find myself wading through a grassy field toward Crystal Creek. I want to see the place where Arthur died. One last time, then I will never go back. This is my final goodbye to him.

I am serious about opening a new chapter to my Book of Life.

Panting to get my breath by the time I get there, I'm grateful my cell phone is tucked inside my pants pocket. I may need a ride back to the house. As I approach the spot where Mark Hagen cruelly struck Arthur on the head with a rock, I pause as my heart stutters.

I am trembling. Maybe, this coming here is a mistake. Maybe I am not ready to say goodbye to Arthur yet. Maybe . . .

Something whizzes by my face. It feels like a bee sting. I touch my cheek with my left hand and feel something soupy. I look at my hand. There's blood on it. Suddenly, I feel dizzy. Then . . .

Then I am on the ground. The weight of someone on top of me. I roll over and push up on one elbow. "Tom?"

"Hi, sweetheart. It's nice to see you today."

I shove Agent Kessler off me and try to get up. But that move doesn't work. He grabs my leg and pulls me to the ground again.

"That was a bullet that grazed your cheek."

"A bullet?" I want to pinch my arm and wake up.

"Someone is trying to kill you, Dorothy."

"Get off me, Tom!" I hiss.

"No." He holds to me like Super Glue. "I know what you did."

"You make it sound like something illegal." I am crawling across the grass with him like we are soldiers in a war. Perhaps we are.

"How did you get here?" I ask.

"Same way as you, I walked."

We are still crawling.

"How much longer do we have to do this?" I ask.

"Until we reach the tree line."

Which takes another five minutes, at least.

I stand up, my back against the trunk of a large oak. Tom corrals me between his strong arms. His face is up close and personal and I panic. He swipes away the blood on my cheek with a thumb.

His tender action is personal flames my desire.

"There, that's better now."

"What are you doing here?" I rasp, mortified.

"Saving your butt again." He grins like this is fun.

"I don't want you saving my butt." I push him away. *Or touching it*, I add in thought. This man is driving me totally insane.

"I was hoping you'd take the black book to the Director's office."

"You were manipulating me again?" I grit my teeth.

"Just asking for your help; no harm done."

"Ha! I met your cohort, Charlie Darby. I don't trust him."

"That's good to hear, because he's dirty."

"What does that mean?" I duck under one arm to distance myself from him. Then another bullet whizzes past my ear.

Tom reins me in.

"What's going on, Tom?"

"Darby is in cahoots with the Russian Mafia. He's on their payroll, has been for a long time. Probably decades. I suspect they approached him before he attended the FBI Academy. That's how foreign entities work. They plant their young people in significant roles."

"Don't tell me this, Tom. Please." I cover my ears.

"You already know too much, Dorothy. They will never let you live under the circumstances. Director Carlton will never see that book. But they know you still have a copy. Where is it?"

"Back at Ellie's. My house," I clarify. "I can get it."

"Is there anyone else who can get it for you?"

"Lorene. We came in her car."

"Call her."

I fumble for my phone in my pants pocket and dial Lorene's number. It rings and rings. "She probably can't hear for all the noise."

"What's going on over at Ellie's?" he inquires.

His cologne makes me want to snuggle against him.

"Hello to Dorothy!" He snaps his fingers. "Pay attention."

"Oh." I come to my senses as Lorene answers her phone. I hold the phone away from my mouth. "What should I say?"

I wait for instructions, putty in Tom's hands.

"What about the children's book you sent me?"

"Ask her to get both books out of your purse and put them in the mailbox," he instructs me. I am stupefied. "Do it!" he orders.

"Uh, Lorene . . ." my cheek begins to hurt worse. Tom swipes away the blood, glaring at me like I might evaporate.

I wonder where the shooter is and why we're still standing here. Then, I find out. Tom leans around the tree and fires three quick shots.

I hear a thud and drop my cell phone on the mossy ground.

"What did you just do?" I inquire.

"I killed the shooter. Focus, Dorothy."

"I'm trying." But I'm failing. This is surreal.

"Dorothy! Dorothy!" I hear a voice coming from the phone.

"Uh, Lorene, I'll have to get back to you." I end the call.

We approach the figure dressed in black wearing a mask. Tom rips the mask away and we see a black man, eyes deadpan. "Dom."

"You know him?" Tom asks.

"I saw him in Ellie's barn some weeks back. Who is he?"

"An assassin who works for the Russian Mafia."

"I think he tried to blow up Lorene's house with us in it," I tell Tom. "There have been several attempts on my life since you left."

He grasps my shoulders and leans close to my face.

"Do you trust me, Dorothy?"

"I do." But I don't know why.

"You have to come with me. Now."

"Okay, we'll go and get my books and you can drive me back to Claire's house. I've had enough partying for one day," I tell him.

"No, I want you to come with me. Away from Columbia."

"No, no, no . . ." I start backing up, terrified.

"Call Lorene back and tell her to put the books in the mailbox."

45

"WHERE IS GG?" JUNE tugs at the hem of her mother's tee shirt.

"Your great grandmother had other plans today," Helen replies.

"Is GG in trouble again?"

Helen kneels to face her young daughter. "I'm sure she's fine. But she sure enjoys creating a drama. It's not something a little girl should worry about." Helen does not know how to explain her grandmother's unorthodox life filled with mysteries and threats of violence.

"Okay. I hope I have some drama one day."

As June skips away, Helen prays that will not happen. Maybe what Dorothy Powell experiences is not contagious or inherited.

"Have you talk to GG today?" Helen queries her mother.

"She's at a picnic with Lorene, at Ellie Simpson's house," Claire replies as she watches Helen fill a big plastic bowl with potato salad.

"June just asked me if GG's in trouble," Helen reveals.

"No, not today. How can she get into trouble at a 4th of July picnic?" Claire chuckles. "Santa Claus has a greater chance. He might slip down at the North Pole and injure himself in the icy snow."

Helen laughs, too. "You're right." She shakes her head. "I worry that June is fascinated with her GG and will one day imitate her."

Claire balks at the idea. "No way, she's a sensible young girl."

"Is she?" Helen questions.

"Okay, I'll call my mother and we'll verify she is fine."

Claire punches in the number and it rings.

"Hello."

The voice does not belong to her mother.

"Who is this? Who has my mother's phone?" Claire inquires.

"This is Lorene Perkins, Claire."

"Why isn't my mother answering her phone?"

"She's not here right now. I don't know where she went," Lorene replies, but does not mention the books she put in the mailbox.

"Okay, when Mama gets back, have her call me."

"Okay, I will."

The call ends. "Where is GG?" Helen asks.

"Only God knows." Claire's a bit concerned that June is psychic.

* * *

"This is ridiculous, Tom. I am not going with you anywhere," I tell him, secretly thrilled to be on a secret-agent mission from the bad guys as we approach a private airport in his vehicle. We are one up on the Russian Mafia. Dom is dead. And Tom and I live another day.

"You said you trusted me." Tom grins as he helps me climb the stairs to a private airplane at the small airport south of Franklin, Tennessee. "I'll explain everything later." He straps me in a seat.

"Don't I get my one call?" I should at least let Lorene know I am not coming back immediately. I want her to drive my Audi to her house while I phone Claire and tell her to get it with my purse.

But that involves two phone calls.

"When are you bringing me back?" I ask Tom as the pilot checks his equipment for takeoff. "I didn't get a chance to pack a bag."

"I know. You won't need one. We have everything you need."

"What does that mean?" The plane lifts off the ground at warp speed and drops my stomach to the ground. "Tell me, Tom!"

"It's not a discussion we should have immediately. Go to sleep."

I feel a prick in my arm, then I am sleepy, then there is nothing.

Time becomes meaningless. I am drifting on clouds and do not care where I am or what I am doing. And then I wake up.

I look to my left out the plane's window. There's only black darkness. On my right sits Thomas Kessler, sleeping like a baby.

I nudge him. "Wake up, Tom. Where are we?"

He stirs and turns his head away from me.

I won't stand for that. "Tom!" I shout.

He scuttles awake. "What, Dorothy! You don't need to scream."

"I think I do. Where are we? What time is it? And when are you going to take me home?" I point a finger at him like I'm the boss.

He settles down again, snuggling in his seat. I look around and see no other passengers. We are not even in the same plane.

"Tom. This is serious. What is going on?"

"Well, Dorothy, life for you is about to change."

"What does that mean, Thomas?" My dander is up.

He shakes his head to clear the cobwebs. "I gave you a sedative so you would sleep. I wasn't sure you were on board with my plan."

"And what exactly is your board plan?"

"Kidnapping you," he says with a grin.

I fist him on the shoulder. "That's not funny."

"I'm glad you feel that way, Dorothy. Which question do you want me to answer first? What time is it, or where are we?"

"Both, if you don't mind." I settle down a bit. "I'm thirsty."

He uncaps a water bottle and gives it to me.

"It's 6 a.m. Russian time, but we're still flying over the Atlantic Ocean, so time will change the farther we travel across Europe."

"Isn't Russia invading Ukraine?"

"We aren't going to Ukraine."

I insanely laugh. "I can't believe you are rattling my cage like this. Take me home. This minute. I demand it. I hate you."

He grasps my hands. His lips wiggle and I know he's repressing a smile. "Look, Dorothy, we both know you love me. Don't pretend anymore. There is no going home anymore. You are with me."

"I am not WITH YOU!" My emotions are exploding and I fear I will have a heart attack and pass out.

"Here." He hands me a billfold. "Look through it."

I see my picture on the Driver's License but I do not see my name. Daphanie Daniels name is on the card. "What is this?"

"Your new I.D. Forget about Dorothy Powell. She does not exist anymore." He says it so calmly I know I am dreaming.

"You jest?"

"Not in the least."

"What about my clothes?"

"I bought new ones for you."

"What if I take medication?"

"You don't. I have antihistamine and Tylenol if you need it."

"I hate you."

"I love you," he says.

"So, we're going to Russia?"

"Yep, and Director Carlton has sanctioned you for a new job with the CIA. You are my secretary and will be financially compensated."

"What about the creep, Agent Charlie Darby?"

"Well, now, that is still a loose end."

I do not understand what that means, but one thing I do know: I am in the middle of something that is going to take some time to unravel in my dizzy mind. But luckily, I do trust Tom.

www.ingramcontent.com/pod-product-compliance
Lightning Source LLC
LaVergne TN
LVHW020824301225
828607LV00008BA/147